The Spiral

by Tabbie Browne

is the sequel to

White Noise Is Heavenly Blue
by Tabbie Browne

ISBN: 978-1-84944-013-4

This book is dedicated to: -

You, the reader.

TABBIE BROWNE ABOUT THE AUTHOR

Tabbie Browne seems to have been writing all her life in one way or another. She didn't have the fear of compositions, later known as essays, at school and would err on the side of writing too much rather than too little.

Although she likes to communicate with people, she has learnt that it sometimes better to sit back and observe the way they act.

She also believes in listening to your vibrations, if you don't get a good feeling when you are with someone, there is probably a good reason for it.

So she follows her instincts much more now, being older and wiser and having found out the hard way that looking for the good in everyone doesn't always pay off.

Copyright © 2009 Tabbie Browne

First Published in Paperback in 2009

Cover Illustrated by Katherine Butler

Apart from any use permitted under UK Copyright law, this publication may only be reproduced, stored, or transmitted, in any form, or by any means, with prior permission in writing of the publishers or, in the case of reprographic production, in accordance with the terms of licenses issued by the Copyright Licensing Agency.

All characters and scenarios in this publication are fictitious and any resemblance to real persons, living or dead, is purely coincidental.

ISBN: 978-1-84944-035-6

British Library Cataloguing in Publication Data.
A catalogue record for this book is available from the British Library.

Published by UKUnpublished.

UKUnpublished
.co.uk

www.ukunpublished.co.uk
info@ukunpublished.co.uk

THE SPIRAL

By

TABBIE BROWNE

CHAPTER 1

The hybrids were dormant. Having been mutilated to perfection during their formation on earth, these Earth/Zargon creatures were kept in readiness for their evil maker's revenge. But not on earth, as the Almighty Powerful One on Eden envisaged.

The first batch of these semi human forms had been transported to a space area near Zargon where they were joined by new arrivals as and when they were produced. Being half human, it would be imagined they would retain some of their human attributes, but continual brain washing by the evil forces soon killed off any trace of anything recognizable.

The large eyes were closed and the thread like silvery grey bodies hung like stalactites, being re-charged at regular intervals. The heads of the newest arrivals were larger, to accommodate more microchips. The workforce on earth had succeeded in continually obtaining all the female eggs they needed to keep the strain going, and the male fertilization was no problem, as the Zargs in human bodies undertook the task willingly.

In his wisdom, Zargot had moved his stock away from the earth to make detection almost impossible. He was aware that Jenny, now fully restored in the ultimate upper spiral on Eden, would not rest until she had traced his source, and attempted yet again to overcome him.

But even in the best, most successful operations, things go wrong. With the evil end product now being churned out with increasing speed, there were inevitably more rejects. The problem arose at the earth station, as to the disposal of these 'seconds'. If too many were merely killed off and dumped, they could be found by the military forces. If incinerated, the ash still had to be spread. Zargot had insisted that only the perfects were dispatched to the holding station, and there was no way a load could be diverted without his knowledge.

That was until one of the evil one's little satellites came up with a brilliant idea. It was so good it worried Zargot. If his underlings were getting too clever, it was time for him to show a few of his powers. He could not risk any more usurpers trying to overthrow him. There were enough of those in his upper spiral, always jostling for supremacy, waiting to claim the ultimate position. This particular worker, known by his earthly name John, wanted to dispose of the rejects by dropping them into an active volcano, live. Zargot recognized this sadistic streak with caution and over-ruled the suggestion immediately. He ruled that a load of live throw outs be dispatched into space and then exploded. That way there would be little or no evidence as their sad remains would soon be burned up.

He was also planning the destruction of the earth base in the near future. It was inevitable that it would be discovered soon, but the greed he felt at the production of his hybrids held him off until the very last moment. The Zargs born into human bodies would have to die of course, and here again, the disposal of their fragile earthly remains would have to be carefully managed.

As with the spirals of the good forces on Eden, Zargon also had a lower spiral of seven beings, all anticipating a climb to the upper spiral and not caring how they did it. The hatred amongst them festered and boiled until the space area became saturated with the ultimate evil. For now, at least, Zargon reigned supreme, which was exactly the way he intended it to continue.

"And how are we today Gladys?" The tone was very patronizing and the speaker did not expect to receive an answer, today, or any other day. Mrs. Randle sat silently in her chair at the nursing home as Lizzie, the carer patted her cushions. Gladys had not seen Jack since just after the fire episode, he could be dead by now for all she knew. Not that she appeared to know much at all. To the outside world she had no mind, no feelings, she could only sit and stare in front of her.

"It's a lovely day today." Lizzie carried on regardless. She was used to speaking to most of the half a dozen patients and not waiting for a reply. Old Joe, on the other hand could talk the hind leg off a donkey, if she gave him the chance. She stroked Gladys's head gently and smiled. "I wonder what she was like, when she was younger" she thought as she left to prepare the afternoon teas.

Lizzie Stokes was a pleasant young thing, not over bright but could get by at a push. She lived just outside Burford, had been to the local school and took the job of carer at the little nursing home on a temporary basis. However, the matron liked her willingness, and when one of the staff left to have a baby, she kept Lizzie on. The patients seemed to like the girl's open friendly manner, even if she was a bit scatty at times. Although they didn't respond much, they appeared relaxed in her presence, which was more than could be said for Vernon, who seemed to put the women on edge. He came in on a part time basis to help with the two male residents, shaving them and talking to them from a man's point of view. The female staff often wondered what went on in these private 'mens meetings' as they were called.

The matron eyed him with suspicion. Given the choice, she would not have employed him, but help of that nature was not easy to come by, and he undertook the unpleasant tasks without complaint. She wondered if he actually enjoyed the messy bits. Apart from the work at the home, he also did odd jobs for people, gardening, handywork, cleaning and somehow managed to eek out a living for himself. He often got a good meal at the home for which he did a few extra jobs. At the age of thirty nine he was single and lived alone. He appeared to have no interest in either the opposite sex or his own. At least, that's what people thought. Old Joe and the other male resident, Pete thought he was a nice enough sort of chap, always friendly, and didn't mind sneaking them into the greenhouse for a crafty cigarette and a glance at a saucy magazine or two. The fact of them doing it behind matron's back seemed to give it all the more spice. This side of him showed the recipients a bit of harmless fun, which is not how one would describe his private activities.

Jenny had re-entered the upper spiral on Eden at the bottom and slowly worked her way up as the upper ultimates were dispatched to tasks on various planets by the Almighty One. Her father, although pleased she had regained almost all of her former talents, was still uneasy with her underlying revenge. "This is not how we work" he would communicate, "we rule by love, not hate." And once again reminded her "You do not bargain or make the rules. You obey."

She was next in line when the order came. As she expected to go to Uranus knowing there had been a lot of trouble with a so called black hole in the area, she was a little surprised to be dispatched to earth to take charge of a portal closing. It could have been any location, but she was directed to a site near Minster Lovell, at a copse set in a hollow and out of view from any nearby roads. The only access was off the main Witney to Burford road, down a track barely visible. Caution was uppermost as Jenny approached, expecting to be met by ideals in earth form. Everywhere was quiet and she was alone. Eventually she saw it, a narrow tornado of green mist rising from the clearing in the centre of the copse. "Looks as though I've got to close this one myself" she thought. This was highly irregular and only done in the most extreme cases. As if in answer she was aware of five figures approaching at speed all covering in the familiar white garb. She held back and let them form a circle around the portal, and when their heads were lowered she took her place at the head position her light radiating from her. Together they squeezed until the opening was raised higher and higher, and she knew it would be dispatched from the greater powers above. This was a small portal compared to some and the six could easily close it. Jenny brushed her hand over the still lowered heads and left instantly, leaving them to return to their earthly lives.

She was about to return to Eden but was halted momentarily by the urge to return to her previous home in Shipton. This was the first time she had re-visited these familiar surroundings on earth and felt the need to be near the wall that had so changed her life. Her mind turned to Matthew as she recounted the physical love they had shared. Existence on Eden was so different, and although she could communicate with those close to her, Matthew, Graham and Marie, she longed for another taste of earthly bliss. Her father, the Almighty One knew of this and was disturbed. He was aware that this could one day be her downfall in the endless fight between good and evil, for was it not the sins of the flesh that were revelled in by Zargot? This was the tool of the evil one, and he would use it.

In an instant she was hovering over the wall overlooking the village. "How naive I must have appeared," she pondered, "but what must Matthew have gone through watching me, fearing he would be recalled when my knowledge returned." She moved slowly down to the cottage where her mother and father still lived. They were a few years older now but the pain etched on both their faces made them appear more so. Jenny too felt the pain as she watched and wished she could ease it for them. Nothing had been changed apart from the framed photographs of her as a child, on her wedding day, and with baby Gabriel which were all around the room. She gently brushed a kiss on their cheeks and returned in thought to Eden.

Kate put her hand to her face and looked to Jimmy for some response, but he sat staring in front of him. As she turned to look at Jenny's picture, the tears flowed once more.

CHAPTER 2

Lizzie was excited. It was Saturday and she was going to the pictures at Witney that evening with a friend.
"Bet it's a fellow." one of the kitchen staff teased her.
"Wrong then." Lizzie tried to be secretive but hadn't quite mastered the art.
"If you must know I'm going with Margaret, my friend, her dad's taking us, then fetching us back."

She later told Gladys all about it, more for something to say than hold a conversation for she knew the woman wouldn't understand a word. Not being the most observant girl in the world, she failed to notice Gladys' eyes fix on her as she busied about. This unseemingly innocent scrap of humanity had been used by Zargot once, and he was quite content to have her situated her for future use. He would visit her body as and when he pleased. This was not a task for any of his underlings; he wanted to reap the full pleasure of his next object which was now standing nicely in his firing line. So the eyes looking out from Mrs. Randle's body were not hers, they were Zargot's. And he was looking straight at Lizzie.

Vernon Treloar had the half day off. He too was going out that night, but for hardly the same pleasures as his workmate. He had a rugged look about him, rather unkempt, his thick brown hair falling in unruly fashion about his forehead. He never seemed to bother about his appearance, and as most people only saw him working, the general impression was of a man who went about his business, but didn't socialize and kept pretty much to himself. He used a push bike for transport which seemed to suit his meager needs.

Now he stood in front of the full length mirror in his bedroom. The curtains were closed and the only light came from a small lamp on the table nearby. Slowly, he absorbed the image of his naked form. No-one would have recognized this handsome upright, very male body, as

the insignificant 'nobody' who would hardly be noticed in a crowd. He had just bathed and was slowly massaging a heady oil into his skin. The hair was sleek, combed back from his face which now took on a slender sculpted almost waxed appearance.
He wallowed in self admiration, turning his shape until he had examined every angle, smoothing his hands over his buttocks, bringing them up to his chest, and then sliding them slowly to his groin. His eyes were molten, his mouth drooling as he whispered "Soon, soon I will have her, soon she will be mine."

Vernon, or Vedron to give him his true name was not one of Zargot's underlings, but almost as deadly. His race came from space area Vex, whose inhabitants were a self centred, self loving lot who bore the human resemblance where ever they travelled. Unlike the Zargs, they look great delight in being seen, knowing they were spreading their nasty little ways amongst the community without being suspected. Their aims were purely on a sexual basis, but the most destructive factors were their jealousy and their possessiveness. What they took for themselves, no other force could have, but if some-one else had something they wanted, they expected to take it. There are still quite a number on the earth today.

And so Vedron donned his apparel for the impending ritual and slipped away into the night.

John viewed the last batch of hybrids to be dispatched to the holding station. There had been a surge of sightings recently and Zargot was ready to close the earth base in the desert before any military snoopers discovered him. There were reports of the usual UFOs and abductions, which were becoming so common place, people fobbed most of them off as publicity seeking.

John was from the lower spiral on Zargon, and like his fellow ideals was more than eager to gain supremacy to the upper spiral knowing full well he would have to oust one of the upper seven to do it. He realized the power in his hands as he viewed the poor wretches before him, all manufactured from his own seed. These would be his. With these in his power, he would climb the ladder to ultimate power, and overthrow even Zargot himself. He, Johhahn would eventually be the most evil force ever known. Then the powers on Eden would really have a fight on their hands. He looked down at the six blank expressions before him. "Soon my children, soon we will rule the upper spiral, and then everything will be in my power."

Unknown to Zargot, these six had been programmed differently. Johhahn had attempted to clone his evil character into each of the creatures, created enough dormant hatred to be triggered when required. Therefore when he eventually took over as ultimate ruler, as he expected, there would be a total of seven like him, but all being him.

His work at the earth station being over, he now prepared to dispose of his body so that no trace could be found. He set about planning the next hours with military precision. Firstly, he would dispatch J1 -J6, his children, to the space area. He would then make a final inspection, destroying all he could. The remaining Zarg workers would be given a lethal injection and incinerated, their ideals returning to their home planet. The earth base, being underground could easily be disposed of without trace, provided nothing was allowed to reach the surface. When all this was completed to his satisfaction, he would release a deadly chemical throughout the complex which would burn all in its path, and lethally inject himself so that his remains would burn with the rest. His ideal could then be thought transported to Zargon. Such was the plan.

Lizzie excitedly waited for Margaret to arrive. "Calm down girl" her mother smiled at her. "You'll burst."

"Oh Mum, I don't go out much, and I've really been looking forward to seeing this film." She patted her hair.

"Do I look alright?"

"You look perfect." The mother fussed around her for reassurance. "Are you sure it's Margaret you're going with?"

"Mother!" her laugh tinkled with merriment, and she pretended to give her parent a little push. The door bell startled them both.

"There you go, have a nice time." Lizzie bent slightly for her mother to kiss her cheek.

"Thanks Mum, you'll be alright won't you?"

"Of course, now be off with you."

The two giggling girls waved to the lone figure on the doorstep. Margaret's dad, called from the car. "Don't worry, I'll bring her back safely, Beth."
"Thank you Robert, very kind of you."
With a lot more waving, Beth watched as the car disappeared from sight then returned to her fireside chair. "I wish her father could have seen her, he'd have been so proud of her." Her thoughts drifted to her late husband, who had only seen the little girl reach two years old before he was killed, knocked down by a car almost on their own doorstep. But Beth wasn't one to be down for long, and taking the chance of being alone, she got up and uncovered a dress she was making for Lizzie for her birthday.

On her return to Eden after closing the portal, Jenny entered the upper spiral from the bottom, awaiting her next assignment. She was aware of areas of unrest in the solar system, and also of problems in other galaxies. The 'helpers' were very busy, pulling in aid from any areas they could. She was never expected to attend disaster areas, as her powers were needed on a higher level, but sometimes, on returning from a task, if she knew Marie was involved, she would stop by and spend some time with her.

Her father took her to task on this. "You have higher powers and your work is directed accordingly. The lower spiral is capable of controlling the transitions, (people passing over) your time should not be diverted where you are not called or directed." His thought instruction was absorbed in a second.
"But is it not right to keep in touch with all that is going on, everywhere?" She would always come up with an answer.
"My child," the thought instruction was not to be argued with. "Why do I have a lower spiral?" There was no pause for a reply. "I have a lower spiral to execute the tasks to which they are specialized. Do you think them incapable of informing me of the true facts?"
"No Father."
"Could they perform your tasks?"
She paused. "Matthew did."

"No." She felt the force behind the thought. "Matthew did not. He occupied your place until you were able to return. He did very well, but he does not have your power, nor would I expect him to."

She was already feeling admonished, but the Almighty One had not finished with her.

"Who else can double thought travel? Who else has overcome the evil one?"

"I know Father. I will do as you wish."

She knew she had not been dismissed.

"You still bear anger and revenge. You know that is against my wishes and our teaching."

"Yes Father. But I feel we should always be ready, just in case."

Again a pause. "That is good, but that is not all. Is it?"

"No."

"You go out to these disasters, these traumas hoping for a lead to it being instigated by Zargot." When she was silent he asked. "Don't you?"

"Yes."

"You know the difference. It is one thing to be prepared, to be on the defense. It is quite another matter to do the attacking."

The meeting was ended.

The Almighty One feared for his child. He knew, even with his continual preaching, she would always continue the fight, even if it destroyed her, but she would not be doing it with love, which to him conquered all.

Vedron stood alone on the winding back lane which ran parallel with the main Burford High Street. It was unlit and the perfect place for the driver of the approaching car to stop and pick him up. In silence he opened the door, placed himself in the front passenger seat and they sped off into the night in the direction of Minster Lovell. The driver and two back seat passengers were also male and were to be met by three others at their destination.

As they approached the barely visible lane leading to the copse, they saw the other vehicle slowly making its way down the track. When they were about a mile from the road, the drivers parked the cars and all passengers got out, each taking a bag. Here they quickly donned long black hooded garments until it was impossible to distinguish one from

the other. Leaving their belongings in one of the cars, they all slowly made their way to the clearing. Vedron was leading the way when suddenly he stopped. "Someone's been here." he whispered.
"How do you know?" came the faint reply from one of the number.
"Look at the portal. Or at least, where it was." All was dark.
He moved forward slowly, switched on his torch, the light covering the ground in the centre of the clearing and scanning the remains of the fire extinguished at the last ritual.
"As I thought." Anger filled his voice. "They've closed it."
"Can't we open it again?" Another one questioned.
"And do you think that to be wise?" Vedron's tone was filled with sarcasm.
"I - m not sure---" the voice trailed off.
"If they have closed it once, they are aware of the position. We will have to find an alternative placing." He started to retrace his steps then stopped.
"Maybe all is not lost. It is a pity to waste the occasion." Everyone fell silent as he mused to himself. "The target I seek is not experienced in our ways. We do not need help to achieve the first goal."

A general bustle of excitement ran through the group at the prospect of not having to abandon the evening completely.
"Light the fire." Vedron's command was immediately obeyed. Soon a makeshift altar was dancing in light from the crackling twigs. The six slowly circled the fire chanting in monotones as Vedron took his place behind the altar, arms up stretched, eyes closed.
"Bring her to me. Bring her to me. Bring her to me." He droned pulling his fingers down through the air and running them down his body to his chest. An image of his desire filled his brain as he raised one arm to the sky. "Give her to me now, that I may fill her body." The eerie sound echoed through the night, but no earthly form outside the gathering was near enough to hear it.

CHAPTER 3

Gladys was in a frenzy, and the night staff were caught unawares by the outburst of this normally docile woman.
"He's after her." She was screaming at the top of her voice.
"Who is Gladys?" the night nurse put her arm around her to calm her but was thrown away with such force she fell to the floor.
"He's after her, poor little thing, don't let him get her." Mrs. Randle was sobbing uncontrollably her eyes wide with fear.
"What IS going on?" Matron appeared and instantly took stock of the scene before her. The night nurse recounted the last few minutes, and as Gladys appeared to be getting more hysterical than ever, Matron decided to ring the doctor who would prescribe a sedative. It had never been necessary before but the poor woman had obviously had a nightmare or something triggered from her past.

When she had been calmed and put to bed, the staff mused as to the cause.
"She was alright at tea time." Matron said. "I wonder when it started."
"As far as I can make out," the young night nurse rubbed her arm, "just before you came in. She seemed asleep then just started yelling."
"Must have been a dream then. Better keep an eye on her tonight. Call me straight away if you have a problem, or if she does it again." Matron got up to go.
"Yes matron."

Zargot had left the poor wretch, he had no use for her tonight. The object of his attentions was out with a friend and that is where he would be; later. But now he thought travelled to the holding station to check the final stages of the storage of his hybrids, now totaling well over five hundred. They all hung in rows, pathetic scraps of his evil invention all receiving their little electrical pulses to keep them ticking over. If one appeared to be weakening in any way, it was given a jolt to 'kick start' it, as Zargot sadistically put it.

It was hard to tell if they actually felt anything, either pain or emotion. They had been so programmed and micro chipped it was almost wrong to attribute them with any earthly connection whatsoever. But that was their origin, so who could ever tell if traces had remained? Could they think? Zargot didn't care, as long as they were ready for when the time came, and then he would rule everything. This time he would not be defeated, especially by HER.

As he traversed the rows he noticed six spaces still empty. The last batch. But why were they not here by now? He began to feel distrust and wondered what Johhahn was playing at. He would have to check for himself and decided to go without form, therefore undetectable. Immediately he thought travelled to the earth station to find the J1- J6 hybrids awaiting dispatch. Johhahn was busy preparing the launch unaware he was being watched as Zargot slipped inside the capsule. He was astonished at the change of format of these last six. There was something very different about them. As he studied them he felt their eyes, which should have been blank, all staring at him with one penetrating glare. Time for answers.

He appeared as though just travelled near Johhahn who carried on with his tasks with little heed to his master.

"Explain." Zargot was curt.

"Explain what?" Johhahn flicked some switches on the console before him.

"Why the difference?"

Johhahn looked at the angry form which was now inches from his face.

"You've never remarked before, and we have been adjusting and amending all along the programme. If we had carried on, there would have been many more improvements." He turned away unflinching.

Zargot eyed him carefully. Either these were the facts, or this was a clever ideal that would have to be watched as he already knew, but for now he would let him have enough rope, so he asked "When will they go?"

"Two hours, twenty three minutes." Johhahn still did not face Zargot but carried on as if he was not there.

"And the workers?"

"It's all arranged, by this time tomorrow there will be no trace of anything."
Zargot stood in front of him. "Then your work here in this form is almost finished. Time for your return to the lower spiral. Well done." The praise was false and the man knew it, for neither trusted the other.

Lizzie and Margaret had enjoyed the film, the night out, and especially each other's company. They had been close friends since junior school and as they both lived in the same area had kept up the association. They shared girlie talk and although both had a bit of an eye for the lads, neither had actually had a boy friend. Margaret had been out with one of the local boys once, but that was about all and Lizzie, sad to say, had never been asked, but she would dream that one day she would meet someone wonderful.

"Is that your dad's car?" She nudged Margaret and indicated in the direction of a dark saloon sitting with its engine running.
"Looks like it." her friend peered into the poorly lit street. "I wonder why he parked right over there."

Slowly they made their way to the car when Margaret stopped suddenly, grabbed Lizzie's arm and said "It's not him" They quickly retraced their steps to the brightly lit cinema foyer. Neither could understand why they had both felt threatened. There were two of them and it was probably some innocent person waiting for a relative. But when Robert pulled up outside, they jumped in the car with such relief, casting a backward look at the other one, which was no longer to be seen.

Margaret's dad laughed. "What's the matter with you two?"
"Nothing Dad" Margaret cut in quickly, but the girls exchanged uneasy glances which neither could explain.

They travelled in silence for a while, then Robert called over his shoulder, "Well, how was the film?"
"Very good Dad," Margaret looked towards her friend who agreed "Oh yes, it was great, thanks." Then after a moment Margaret leaned forward and said quietly, "Dad, when you came for us, did you notice another car like ours, parked near the cinema?" Lizzie gave her a stern look, wishing she had not mentioned the event in case it was only their imagination.
"No, can't say I did. Why?"

"Oh nothing," Margaret tried to make light of the query, "just that we thought it was you."
Robert gave a short laugh. "Oh, my lift not good enough eh? Nearly went off with someone else did you?"
Lizzie was rather uneasy. "No, it wasn't like that, I'm sure it was just a mistake."
The dad shrugged. "Sorry ladies, I can't help you with that one."
They carried on making small talk about the film, more to break the silence than out of interest.

They left the outskirts of Witney and were heading back along the A40 towards Burford. They had just passed the Minster Lovell turn, the lights of the car cutting into the blackness, when Robert braked suddenly. There straight in front of him was a lone man waving frantically.
"Stay here" Robert yelled at the two girls. "I'll see what the matter is."
As he got out of the car the man beckoned wildly. "Quick, we've run off the road, you must help."

With only the lights of his own car, Robert instinctively followed the man in the direction of what he believed to be an accident. As soon as he was engulfed in darkness, he was seized by two of Vedron's helpers, one holding a cloth to his nose and mouth until he became unconscious. Vedron moved to the car and the two worried friends.
"I'm sorry, we've had an accident, your friend is helping."
"That's my Dad" Margaret cut in.
"Sorry," the voice was lilting as Vedron knelt on the front passenger seat facing the two girls in the back, "I don't know what we would have done if you hadn't come along."

Lizzie had the uneasy feeling she knew this voice and its owner. She had not recognized Vedron in the gloom as the odd job man, Vernon with whom she worked. She could easily be forgiven, even if she had seen him in full light, for he bore little resemblance to his daily appearance. But there was something, a nagging, tormenting her to remember as his voice lulled them both into a deep hypnotic trance. He got out of the car, turned and beckoned his two henchmen, who arrived and bundled Robert's body into the passenger seat. One then jumped into the driver's seat whilst Vedron and the other climbed into the back with the girls.

"Quick, get this out of sight," he snapped as they bumped down the track to where the other cars were hidden.

"What will we do with him?" The driver referred to Robert.

"Leave him. He won't wake up yet. We have long enough." They all got out leaving the girls sprawled out on the back seat. Vedron again started to speak in low tones, ordering the two to do as he bid. Very mechanically, they got up, eyes bearing a far away look, and followed him to the clearing.

A slight whisper ran through the rest of the group when they saw two maidens. A bonus. But Vedron held up his hand to silence them as he led the two females to the altar. He placed them in front and he took up his position behind, facing the assembled group. At a signal, two followers moved forward and began to undress the girls. Vedron could easily have made them do it themselves, but this gave more satisfaction to all onlookers.

After a moment of incantation, he instructed Lizzie to lie on her back upon the altar. His hands high he gave thanks for her having been brought to him. "This is mine." he almost roared, then pointing to Margaret he almost spat the words, "You can all have her, but you do not touch this."

Eagerly the six scrambled forward all wanting to be first, the frustration aching in their groins, knowing relief was in their grasp. Margaret was grabbed, mauled and thrown upon the ground, all of them pawing her every opening. Vedron let them have their will, as he knew, that with providing them with a plaything of their own, he could take his time in satisfaction of his achievement.

He had planned this operation in detail, knowing the girls' movements, for Lizzie shared her arrangements with anyone who would listen. And Vernon Treloar had certainly listened. He had not considered it necessary to divulge everything to the lower beings, and they found out when the time was right so that was sufficient.

Casting his gaze over the scene before him, he now turned his attention to the task in hand. The rape of Lizzie.

CHAPTER 4

"The portals on Earth are being re-opened as fast as you are closing them." The thought message descended from The Almighty Powerful One through the upper spiral and down to the lower. "I am afraid this extra activity is dangerous two fold. Not only could we have a concentrated in surge of evil in one area, but in fighting it our attention could be drawn away from a greater occurrence elsewhere."

Jenny sent her reply through the spirals.

"This is what I was afraid of. I believe Zargot to be behind it, which means he is planning something big, but preparing it elsewhere in the universe."

The Almighty One immediately intervened. "Do not make the mistake of thinking only Zargot is capable. I am not reprimanding you daughter, only warning you not to be tunnel visioned. Open your minds, all of you. Yes, Zargot could be behind most things, he is the Ultimate Ruler over all evil, BUT, he could be working through willing sources, not the Zargs."

Marie offered, "There are always those trying to take his place, not only in his own spirals."

"Correct, you see much of the result of evil, as do your helpers." The Almighty One always admired Marie's calmness. Pity Jenny hadn't more of her qualities, but on the other hand could Marie have got the better of the evil one as skillfully as his daughter had?

With a blessing the conference was ended.

Matthew and Graham had been dispatched to do a sweep as it was called. This entailed covering the active areas of the earth to detect possible portals or centres of evil concentration. The information would then be fed back for one of the more powerful upper spiral to deal with.

They often wondered if the same operation was used by Zargot to find the 'good spots'.

Voodoo and witchcraft were still rife in certain parts of the world, and held a powerful hold on the believers. In extreme cases some poor creatures actually died of shock. This fuelled the fear amongst their families and friends who were then too afraid to go against the tyranny which ruled their lives. Equally there were as many good forces, but as people were not made to fear good, or live in terror of its wrath, it did not receive quite the same publicity. Nevertheless, still an unseen force to be reckoned with.

Having covered Haiti and most of Africa, the two ideals moved up through Europe until they were about to sweep England. There were still many covens active in the rural areas although some were not too much of a threat. However, experience had taught the two never to eliminate a seemingly innocent activity, for these could be the little seeds just waiting to be nurtured.

Jenny wished she could have accompanied Matthew and Graham but knew that was impossible. She could only follow up anything they uncovered, if she happened to be the next in line in the upper spiral when the call came. Also to deal with it alone, unless it was too big, and needed a reinforcement of strength, which in her case was rarely necessary.

For a moment, Zargot's interest was directed towards an earthly source. Through the eyes of Gladys Randle, he had observed Lizzie's every working movement and, through the girl's friendly banter, had learned of her plans for that evening. He was ready to move in and begin to manipulate her to his needs, slowly at first, until she was under his power and only too ready to please him.

So, when he observed Vedron's attentions, the fury welled up swamping his ideal. The indignity of it! To think a lesser power like a Vexon could walk in and take what he had planned for himself. But something made him stop. Had he been in physical form, a sly smirk would have spread across his face. Instead he hovered invisible above the scene in the clearing, savoring for a moment the abuse of Margaret, then letting his concentration swing across to where Vedron was about to enter Lizzie for the second time.

One of the disadvantages of being in physical state, is that any extreme power, good or bad, can take over, use the vehicle for it's purpose, and then leave, usually undetected and leaving no trace or knowledge.

In a flash, Zargot had taken over Vedron. He felt his strong arms at full stretch, one hand either side of Lizzie's head her tousled hair tumbling from the altar. He looked down into her simple face but she did not see him. The eyes were still glazed looking far away in her hypnotic trance. As the earthly feeling swept through his body, he was instantly aware of the frenzied arousal in his lower part. He rammed himself inside her, ripping her virgin membranes and planting his own thoughts into her mentally drugged brain.

Satisfied, he immediately withdrew from Vedron who put this strange feeling down to exotic sexual stimulation. Zargot watched, unseen, as Vedron collapsed exhausted on top of his prey, his body spent. Even he was astounded at 'his' performance. This was the best he had ever experienced, and yet there had been no response from the girl now lying squashed beneath him. He had raped her, taken her for his own lust and jealous possession and would return her to her normal little humdrum life without her even being aware of his true self.

Slowly he withdrew and climbed off her. The other six were just about finished with Margaret and had taken little notice of their leader, being too intent on enjoying themselves. A slight fracas began over who had possessed her the most, the jealousy now rearing, the pleasures being over. Vedron called the assembly to order. "Get her cleaned up" he snapped. One of them came over to the altar. Vedron held him at arm's length.

"And just where do you think you are going?"

The man shrank back a little. "Thought you might need help with that one."

"Did I not make myself clear? No one touches that." His long finger stabbed the air in the direction of his conquest. "That is mine, and mine alone." With a quick nod, the other turned and hastened back to attend to Margaret.

Zargot viewed this with amusement. "So you think she is yours you pathetic rat. We shall see." And he instantly departed to make a personal inspection on his hybrids.

Beth was getting a little worried. Even if the film hadn't finished until half past ten, Lizzie should have been back by now. She glanced at the clock. Eleven fifteen. She felt the grip of apprehension rise in her stomach. Perhaps if Lizzie had always been the sort to go out, she wouldn't have worried so much, and perhaps if she had not been the only one she wouldn't have been so bothered.
"Oh perhaps, perhaps, what good is this doing" she paced from the table to the door.
"I know," she spoke aloud, "if they're not back in five minutes, I'll ring Robert's wife." She didn't fancy the prospect, as Madge Bradley was not the friendliest of women. Many felt sorry for Robert being tied up with such a person, and it was believed she had trapped him into marriage, when all the time he would have preferred Beth. This had always left a bad taste and Beth tended to keep her distance unless absolutely necessary.

"Well," she decided, "this is when it is absolutely necessary." But, still being tempted to put it off until the very last moment, she thought, "They could be there. Perhaps Robert took Lizzie back to their place for a drink or something to eat." But the idea faded just as quickly. Firstly he would know Beth would be worried, and secondly Madge would hardly make her girl welcome.

"I'll give it till half past, and then I WILL ring." Satisfied with the decision she sat down to watch the clock tick away. But the situation was solved for her with the ringing of the telephone. It was Madge.
"You don't happen to have my husband there do you?" The tone was curt.
Beth felt a little angry but paused slightly before replying. "Hello Madge, I was about to ring you. Lizzie isn't back yet."
"Oh." The tone held surprise. "I thought they might have called in to you, it's getting very late."
"I am aware of that, and I am very worried. Do you suppose they could have had an accident?"

"Well, it won't be Robert's fault, he's very careful you know." Even in a situation like this she had to make her point. Whereas Beth was worried for the safety of them all, this woman could only make her snide little jibes.

"Should we call the police?" Beth felt that in a minute she would loose her cool.

"And tell them what exactly?" Madge sounded as if she was dealing with someone else's problem. Nobody would have thought it was her husband and her daughter that were involved.

Beth swallowed. "The facts Madge. They should have been back at least half an hour ago. I'm very worried."

"Very well. I suppose they will want the registration number of the car and everything. This is very tiresome; I shall have something to say to that man of mine when he does finally roll in." She couldn't resist the dig about Robert being hers which was very unkind considering the untimely and tragic death of Beth's husband. But that was Madge all over.

In a resigned tone she promised to call the local police and very condescendingly reminded Beth to let her know if they should turn up in the meantime. Beth slammed down the receiver. "That woman," she seethed, "why did Robert have to end up with her?" the anger being fuelled by increasing worry over her missing daughter.

CHAPTER 5

Lizzie and Margaret had been instructed to return to the car and get into the back seat, still in a tranced state. As the party reached the vehicle, Robert was beginning to come round from the effects of the chloroform and trying to get out of the car. Vedron halted the group and went to him. Quickly he hypnotized him so he would remember nothing, then two of the followers manhandled him into the front passenger seat. Having quickly changed into their normal clothes, Vedron indicated for one of them to drive the car to the road and wait with the lights off. He and the others got into their two cars and followed.

At the main road, they waited until it was absolutely clear of traffic, then they placed Robert's car at an angle as though it had run off the road. Vedron instructed him to sit in the driver's seat. Very quietly he told them all they would wake up in five minutes, also they would remember nothing of the night's true events, and instead all would recall dazzling headlights which had obviously made the driver swerve.

He checked the road, and when satisfied they were alone, beckoned the cars out on to the carriageway. Casting a final look round, he switched on the lights of the now abandoned car, then joined his friends to return to their normal lifestyle.

The United States military had been using their high tech equipment to scan part of a central desert following reports from patrolling jets of strange sightings. It was all very much under wraps. The last thing they wanted was to be invaded by a host of journalists and nosey sight seers, trampling all over the place. Also, they were not prepared to speculate on matters for which they had no proof. There were no known tests being carried out in that precise place, therefore any activity could only be from a source foreign, or worse extra terrestrial.

Two patrolling jet pilots had reported seeing small metallic objects rising from the ground, then speeding upwards until they were out of sight in seconds. It all happened so quickly, they even wondered if they had imagined it, or put it down to a trick of the light. But they had both witnessed the same thing, and one even stated a count of six craft, if that's what they were. The two men were subjected to intense grilling, and kept isolated even from their families. So the military forces were obviously taking their findings seriously.

Other jet patrols were dispatched to the area, although it was difficult to pin point the exact spot. There were no visible signs on the ground, no radar, no equipment, no landing or take off place. It began to be taken as a joke amongst the pilots, but the higher officers were not so sure and had therefore ordered a full search, if only to close the books on the matter.

Johhahn was ready to destroy all traces of the earth base, having dispatched his 'children' to their holding space. He was extra cautious after Zargot's visit, not trusting his ultimate ruler, but distrust was rife in the upper and lower spirals of the Zargs. He smiled to himself, satisfied that he was one step ahead of his lord, holding a trump card to be used as and when he was ready. He moved quickly around the base shutting down all the consoles and units until he stood, needle poised to end his mortal life. Concern filled him that Zargot would start examining his special ones before he could get to them, and realizing his intentions he must delay no further

The chemical was ready for release. Johhahn stood with his free hand on the control.

But even the best laid plans can backfire by one single check being overlooked. When the last hybrids had been dispatched, the launch door had closed, almost. One tiny chink of air had been filtering through the gap and altered the balance of the atmosphere in the underground capsule.

Johhahn, as soon as he had hit the control button, would then inject himself. Death would be instantaneous, hence the order of sequence. As the contact was made, the change in air caused the chemical to back track, engulfing him before he could take his life. As it ate into everything in its path, his tortuous screams echoed through the corridors, while his body burned beyond recognition.

As his ideal rose, free from the remains, it could not discard the memory of the horror so easily, and when he eventually arrived on Zargon the word had preceded him, and he was met with the mental jibes of those on the lower spiral. They revelled in his so called incompetence, and although his ideal was at a low ebb, he knew that one day he would rule all, then they would not laugh so loudly.

The telephone rang and Beth was there in an instant. It was Madge, although it didn't sound like her. The voice was small and strained as she whispered "Beth, they are here. The police are coming to fetch you - "and her voice trailed off into a sob.

"Madge, Madge, what has happened?"

"I don't know, but something - oh Beth, Lizzie's been --" again the muffled sobbing.

"Tell me." Beth was demanding, almost hysterically to know what had happened. "Is she hurt?"

"Upset more than anything, but Beth, she's bleeding or has been?"

"Where? Oh no." The truth was hitting her.

Madge went on. "That's why the police want you here. They think she's been----" there was a silent pause. "And they suspect Robert."

"WHAT?" Beth was trembling so much she fell onto the nearest chair, "No Madge, he wouldn't, he couldn't, I don't believe it. Wait a minute, what does Lizzie say?"

"She can't remember, none of them can, except---"

A sharp knock on the door interrupted the conversation.

"Madge, I think the police are here. I'll see you in a minute." She hung up and flew to the door.

A grim faced woman officer stood on the doorstep. "Mrs. Stokes?"

Beth swallowed hard. "Yes, that's me. How's Lizzie, I must go to her."

The woman did not move. "May I come in for a moment Mrs. Stokes?"

"But I want to see her, I thought you'd come to take me." She was becoming hysterical by now.

The officer's tone softened a little. "I just want a word before we go; it's easier if you know first." Her head tilted to one side in question. "OK?" Beth nodded and stood to one side. "You'd better come in." She knew she would get no satisfaction until she relented.

They both sat facing each other and the policewoman began quietly. "I'm WPC Bell, Mrs. Stokes, I've just seen your daughter and she is unhurt."

"Oh thank God." Beth let out a sigh of relief which was just as quickly replaced with a mother's instinct. "But what has happened? Madge said something about her bleeding. Was it, --you know, --down there?"

WPC Bell nodded. She looked much kinder now. "We think she and her friend Margaret have been raped."

The cry that left Beth bore no words, but it held the fear all mothers have, no matter what the age of the girl.

"Tell me," her voice shook, "Madge said you suspect Robert, that's Margaret's father, but he would never do anything like that. It must have been somebody else."

"We don't know yet, but he appears to have been the only person with them all night, and we have to eliminate every angle. I just wanted to warn you, out of Lizzie's hearing, so that you know what to expect, without the explanations. You understand?"

"Yes, yes, I see."

"The girls will have to be examined by a police surgeon." The officer said it quietly, knowing the effect the news would have on the mother.

"What?" Beth trembled.

WPC Bell continued, "With their permission of course. They are both old enough to decide that for themselves, and they may or may not want you present."

"Oh." This was becoming more horrible the more the truth sank in. Beth wiped her eyes on a hanky.

"There is one other thing." The officer had moved closer to comfort the mother. "Mr. Bradley will not be at the house. He has already been taken to the police station. You see, he has admitted raping Lizzie."

"What? No. I don't believe it. Only Lizzie?" Beth was becoming hysterical again, her brain frantically searching for a logical explanation "And so who, tell me, is supposed to have raped Margaret?"

"Look, it's too early to say, we can only go on what we know up to now."

"Can we go?" Beth was already on her feet.
"Of course, I have a car outside." The WPC waited for the mother to gather a coat, handbag and keys and escorted her to the car.

CHAPTER 6

Jenny was next but one at the top of the upper spiral on Eden when the order came to examine the site in the American desert. She wished she could have gone but the rules of the Almighty One had to be obeyed.

If, as was suspected, the area producing the hybrids had been traced, she felt it her right, in light of all her previous work, to be in at the findings. But her Father in his wisdom had another task for her, equally compelling, but she must wait for a moment.

Reports had filled the newspapers worldwide of strange sightings over the desert base. Following the lights of the dispatched crafts containing the hybrids, the word had somehow leaked to the press, the last thing the military wanted. Therefore, they were all on hand, ready and waiting.

The aperture left by the launch door not closing created a window on the world, and, at the release of the chemical, some had escaped from the chambers to above ground. Being heavier than the surrounding air, it dropped until it spread like an acrid carpet, covering the desert with a deadly weapon. Although colourless, it appeared from the air like a heat haze, distorting the ground as it travelled.

The military were very worried. Not as to how they would contain such a thing, but the fear of world panic as the news leaked. Now the position had been established, they would be inundated with people putting their lives, and those of their families at risk just to say they had been to the place.

As they were setting the clean up operation into practice, Jason, the ultimate from the higher spiral, arrived. He immediately ignored the ground surface and descended into the devastated crypt like chamber, or what was left of it. A quick search confirmed the destruction which had been so carefully planned, and he was about to leave when something caught his attention. In the charred surroundings he found the imprint of what, according to the shape, could only have once been a human.

As he thought returned to Eden he pondered. Immediately a conference was in session. The upper powers wondered why Zargon should have left one of his beings to perish, although it was presumed he would have self destructed the creature first. But if that had been the case, the imprint would not have been in the place or position in which it had been found.

"It would have been more organized," Jenny offered. "Something went wrong."

Her Father sent the thought. "That is obvious, the more we examine the facts.

I believe it was meant to be contained, but somehow there was an escape."

Jason added "The door. Something was wrong with the door."

The Almighty One paused. "Maybe. Or was that how HE planned it?"

Jenny ventured, "But that doesn't make sense Father. If Zargot was behind this, and it looks that way, he knew the ideal would return to Zargon, so what did he achieve by torturing him here?"

"Wise observation." The Almighty One was about to bring the session to a close. "But we know what the evil ones are like. Maybe Zargot didn't trust the underling. Maybe there was a score to settle."

"Deliberate? That makes it all the worse." Jason mused.

"It is a possibility to be considered." With the final thought the Almighty retreated.

As Beth entered the Bradley abode, Lizzie ran to her, throwing her arms around her neck and sobbing.

"It's alright, I'm here now." Slowly Beth calmed her daughter, then looked around the room. Madge stood taut, a large whisky in her hand, whilst Margaret was huddled in the corner of the sofa. The policewoman could not help but draw the comparison between these two couples.

"What happens now officer?" Beth whispered.

"If you are ready ladies, we will go to the police station where the surgeon is waiting."

A cry broke from Lizzie but she bravely said "It's for the best isn't it?"

"It would help." WPC Bell was trying to make it as easy as she could. Madge downed her drink, slammed the glass on the table, harder than she meant to and turned to face the officer.

"And what about my husband?"

"Don't worry madam, you or the girls will not see him, at least not until afterwards. It depends on the findings."

It was a sad little party that left the house, all with mixed and confused feelings.

Lizzie, although hypnotized by Vedron to forget the night's happenings, had received images placed by Zargot during his possession of the Vexon's body. She was getting little flashbacks, but could not piece them together, but she was certain in her own mind that Robert Bradley had nothing to do with it.

Margaret was still almost in a tranced state, as, in her case, the hypnotism had not been overridden, and although she felt agonizingly sore, she did not remember why.

Madge was still grim faced, casting accusing glances at Beth as though it was all her fault, and in some way Beth knew she was blaming her. Her first instinct was for Lizzie, and being a caring mother, for Margaret. She felt pity for the girl, who was getting little enough from her own mother.

After a short conference, it was decided that the police woman would be present during the examination Lizzie was content not to have her mother upset any more than possible, and Margaret just didn't want Madge there.

"She's still very shaken," WPC Bell tried to explain to Madge who turned her back, wishing she didn't have to be dragged into this sordid business.

When the unpleasant task was over, they all wanted to go back home as quickly as possible, but the duty sergeant asked them to wait a moment.

"Haven't we waited long enough?" Madge's voice was slow and precise. The surgeon, accompanied by the ever faithful WPC Bell, entered the room.

"Could I just have a word?" It was not really a question, and he beckoned them into a side room.

"I may have some good news." He directed the remark at the mothers. "Of course, we will have to send off the girls' samples to be absolutely sure, but it is highly unlikely that Mr. Bradley could have --" he nodded at Lizzie.

"I just know he didn't do it." she said in a feeble voice.

Beth put her arm around her. "What makes you so sure Lizzie?"

"I can't say, I - I - know something happened," she turned to the surgeon, "it did didn't it?" he nodded "but oh don't ask me how, but it wasn't your dad Margaret, I just know."

Madge was getting more impatient. "Well of course it wasn't, we all know that, but what are you going to do about finding the real culprit?"

WPC Bell spoke. "Mrs. Bradley, I think you are forgetting something."

"Oh? What pray?"

"Your husband admitted it."

There was silence for a moment, and then the surgeon went on. "Without going into the details, I don't believe he could have, also, having examined him, there was a lingering odour on his breath."

Madge didn't wait for any further explanation. "He had been drinking. Is that what you are trying to say?"

Beth had had enough. "Oh for goodness sake Madge let the man finish." Then to the doctor, "I'm sorry, do go on."

"Quite alright. No, the smell was chloroform."

"Chloroform!" they all cried in unison.

The policewoman leaned towards the girls. "Do try and remember what happened. Anything."

Margaret shook her head and started crying again, ignored by her mother.

Lizzie's faced screwed up a little.

"Yes?" The officer had the glimmer of hope with this one.

"I'm not sure, there was something, but it comes and goes."

"Don't worry for now. It may come back slowly. You've obviously had a nasty shock; it may take a little time." The surgeon rose to go. "I'll be in touch" he said.

"Thank you doctor." WPC Bell saw him out then turned to the ladies. "We will take you all home now."

"And what about my husband?" again the 'my husband' dig from Madge.

"We are letting him go for now, but there are other officers who may wish to speak to him in the morning."
It was Beth who let out the sigh of relief. "Oh thank God." She ignored the cutting look she received from the other woman.

Zargot was pleased with himself. His work was being done for him all around the world. The rot was beginning to fester in little batches, slowly spreading until it would encompass all. He intended to rule, not only the world, but the universe, the galaxies and beyond. He thrived on the power he had already acquired, but much always wants more. And Zargot wanted it all.

He did not trust his ultimates, and always checked everything for himself, which had proved essential when he considered the little games Johhahn thought he was playing on the earth base. But he had sorted that one. The Almighty One on Eden had been correct in calculating Zargot's evil, knowing that, if he so much as suspected treachery, he would deal with it.

The evil one knew Johhahn was up to something, although he hadn't quite fathomed what, but he would be ready. For now he had just given him a little taste of what it was like to cross him. The returning ideal was smarting from the mental pain not suspecting his ruler of being responsible, but blaming a fault in the equipment. Zargot wallowed in such folly.

CHAPTER 7

In his home, Vernon Treloar stood looking at his reflection in the mirror. He now looked more like the odd job man familiar to the staff at the nursing home. Musing over the pleasures of the evening, he had a peculiar nagging feeling and the question going over and over in his mind "What was so different?"

There had been many girls before, the cult meetings were nothing new to his race and the females hypnotized to respond to his every vile wish. He always savoured every last moment, remembering. That was it. "Remembering". He almost shouted to himself. "I can't quite remember the final moments as I took her again. Why?" The only explanation affording itself was that he was so over aroused it had produced this euphoria, which for some reason had never happened before. Had he known the real reason, he would have had much cause for concern.

The seething jealousy began to rise. She was his. Nobody else must touch her. It didn't occur to him that nobody else particularly wanted her, but such was the Vexon characteristic that he could only crave, and possess.

It was Sunday Morning. Madge and Robert were having breakfast, Margaret yet to join them, when they were disturbed by the door bell.

"Now who on earth can that be at this hour?" Madge made her way to the door. "And on a Sunday as well. Yes?" She opened the door to face two plain clothes policemen.

"Good morning madam, I'm Detective Chief Inspector Jones, and this is Detective Sergeant Williams."

"Well?"

"Mrs. Bradley?"

"Yes, what do you want?" Madge's usual impatience was showing.
"Is Mr. Bradley in?"
Robert appeared at his wife's side. "I'm Robert Bradley, what can we do for you?"
"May we come in?"
"Robert moved Madge to one side, "Of course, sorry were having breakfast."
As the two men entered he said "Madge, I'm sure the officers would like a fresh cup of tea." Her response was to glare from him to them and back. Seizing the opportunity of talking to Robert alone, Det. Ch.Insp Jones said "That would be very welcome, thank you," leaving Madge no alternative but to depart to the kitchen, much to her disgust at missing the conversation.

Robert indicated for the men to sit, and left them to open the conversation.
"I expect you can guess why we are here." The senior officer started.
"It's about last night isn't it?" Robert was a little wary.
"Yes, but not in the way you are thinking."
Robert looked from one to the other. "I don't understand."
The sergeant spoke for the first time, "We have been following up some varied enquiries recently, and we think you may be able to help us."
"Oh?"
The younger officer continued. "I'm based locally, but Det.Ch.Insp.Jones has been brought in from Oxford especially because of what happened to you."
Robert still looked bemused. The older man continued.
"Det. Sergeant Williams has been doing some rather specialized investigations, as have other officers in many other parts of the county. I am trying to pull it all together, so to speak."
At this point Madge returned with the tea. "Well?" she enquired, "what's it all about?"
Robert said "I think we are just about to get to that."
Det.Ch.Insp.Jones took his tea and placed it on a small table. "What do you know of witchcraft?"
"Witchcraft!" Robert and Madge chorused.

"It's rife round here. The sergeant here has a file full of reports, some almost on your doorstep. And some" he paused to let it sink in "almost identical to your experience last night."

"But what has witchcraft got to do with my husband?"

"That" said the Ch.Insp. "is what we are here to find out."

The sergeant said quietly "That is why they let you go last night; the duty sergeant recognized the signs and got on to us straight away."

"Signs? What signs?" Robert scratched his head.

"Your breath had chloroform still remaining. You were obviously doped so that the girls could be used for some ritual or other." Det. Sgt Williams turned to Madge. "I'm sorry to ask, but to the best of your knowledge was your daughter a virgin?"

Madge sat for the first time. "Well of course, what sort of girl do you think she is?"

Robert intervened. "They just need to know I expect." Then turning to the officers he asked. "That's important is it?"

The senior man said "Yes, but it's only what we expected, you see they like them, pure, untouched. I expect your daughter's friend is the same." He tried to keep off the official terminology knowing how delicate it was.

"Just a minute." Robert held up his hand. "Are you saying the girls were taken, you know, raped in front of me?" The horror showed on his face.

"We don't know. Not the details, you see the girls can't remember. There is no sign of them being drugged so they were probably put in a trance to make them do - whatever." Det. Sgt. Williams was getting round to the unpleasant bit.

"Mr. Bradley, I know this is painful for you but we have to eliminate all avenues in a matter as serious as this."

Robert felt he wouldn't like what was coming.

"Mr. Bradley, have you or anyone you know every practiced anything to do with devil worship?"

Robert jumped to his feet. "What are you saying? That I had a part in this?"

Det.Ch.Insp.Jones said calmly "Please sit down Mr. Bradley. We are not accusing you. But if something of this nature has taken place, and we strongly believe that it has, we have to start at the beginning and move outwards."

Robert was shaking. "I'd never touch them, and I'd never take part in that sort of act. It's abhorrent."
Madge had been silent long enough. "So what are you doing about it?"
"We've been watching certain places." The Det.Ch.Insp. continued, "one of which is not far from where you were found. They'll probably desert it now, they usually do if we get too near."
The sergeant spoke again. "The reason we are here, is we need your help. Anything you can remember. Any little scrap you can recall. A name. A certain voice. A nickname. A stutter. Anything that could identify at least one."
Robert felt a little easier. "Oh I see, yes. But it's all a blur."
"It may come back, if it does, this is my number, and I'll give you Det.Ch.Insp.Jones number as well, in case you can't get me. And don't forget, anything, however small. It may tie in with something else we have."
"That's right," his superior added as he got up from the chair, "it might not be important to you, but it may match up."

They made their way to the door, bid the Bradleys farewell and were gone.
"At least they believed me," Robert sank onto a chair at the table,
"And why shouldn't they?" Madge poured him another cup of tea.

As the two detectives left the house, the local sergeant asked "Well, what do you make of him?"
"Hmm. Could be telling the truth, "was the reply "if he's aware of what it is. Or he's clever. Keep an eye on him."
"Willdo." The sergeant unlocked the car and they both sped off to the next similar enquiry near Bourton.

Marie had just returned from a space area near Saturn. Another helper had noticed unusual craft in the area of Zargon and reported to her. It appeared they were performing practice flights, and then returning to a small asteroid just off the main planet. Remembering the one that had crashed on its journey to earth, Marie felt there was an uncanny resemblance, and soon alerted the ultimate powers in the upper spiral on Eden. Jenny immediately requested to double switch to the area and survey any activity. She was not at the top of the spiral and therefore not due to be dispatched to the task, but as she was the only one capable of the double switch, the Almighty One granted her leave, warning her it could always be a trap to draw her away, thus leaving the spiral vulnerable.

Within seconds she was back. "I need longer" she thought. "There are several asteroids in the area. I have to detect which is the one in use." On the third attempt she found it, and almost remained longer to examine the area. But caution reigned and she returned immediately. Elated, she spread the word through the spirals and soon a conference was in session.

"They are there, hundreds of them, the poor wretches "she imparted, and felt the surge of sorrow through the spirals, "it surely must be the main holding station, unless he has others, but I don't think there would have been time to 'manufacture' many more." She sent the thought of what she had witnessed, row upon row of blank expressions on the faces of the dangling scraps, whose origin was from the human source. She decided then that she would not rest until the creatures had been released from Zargot's tombs. The Zombies, the living dead.

The next question was "Where are they being groomed for?" The obvious answer to Jenny was earth, after all they had been conceived there, and remembering Jenny's and Marie's connection, it seemed inevitable that was the target.

"There doesn't seem much human in them," Jenny felt sadness at the plight of these wretches. "I hope they don't know anything, for their sakes."Marie thought "I can't help wondering-----" when Jenny's thought cut across "If there are any of our eggs still in them. Don't think. That is what he is hoping for."

Matthew had been observing all this then he offered, "How do you propose to destroy these unfortunate things? By human means?" Jenny was ready with the reply "Any way we can. If it is a question of interrupting their electrical power, the Schynings may be useful."

The conference was ended.

The doctor packed away his stethoscope and closed his bag. "She's gone alright matron. Not a peaceful end by the look of it." Matron looked at Gladys Randle's lifeless form. "Poor thing, she did seem troubled. We thought something was bothering her, but we couldn't make out what it was." They made their way to the office where the doctor started to fill out the necessary forms.

"I'll have to inform the coroner, and there will be a post mortem."

Matron eyed him quizzically. "Something wrong?"

The doctor carried on writing, head lowered. "Maybe. I'll arrange for the removal of the body."

"I don't know of any relatives." Matron continued, "There was a husband, but he had left his last address and we don't know of his whereabouts. Perhaps the police could make some enquiries."

"Oh I think they'll be doing that alright," the doctor gathered his papers together.

"What are you saying doctor?"

Ignoring the question he continued "Please make sure nobody goes into the room, until the police have been."

"But-but- are you saying it was unnatural causes?"

"I'm not saying anything, yet. We will have to await the reports."

He left briskly leaving a stunned matron turning all the possibilities over in her mind. "Was he saying she was---- no. That's impossible." Gathering her wits, the professional side returned and she hastened to lock the door to Gladys's room.

CHAPTER 8

"Are you sure you want to go to work Lizzie?" Beth stroked the girl's hair lovingly.
"Yes please Mum. I've had a day off already and matron's been very understanding, but I've got to get it over with."
"If you're sure dear. It's probably for the best, and the sooner we can put this business behind us, the better."
"Mum, you don't think people will blame me do you?"
"How can they?" Beth was adamant, but then "oh wait a minute; you're worried, not about the truth, but what some of them will make of it?"
"Well, "Lizzie hesitated for a moment, "Margaret's Mum was saying-----"
"Ah" Beth jumped on this "I might have known. Well Lizzie, you ignore the likes of her. Everyone's not the same you know" and she gave her daughter a reassuring hug, but knew that there were only too many willing to believe the dirt. But why worry the girl unnecessarily?

So Lizzie set off for work, little expecting the news awaiting her about Mrs.Randle's sudden death.

The scene in Beth's home was in stark contrast from the Bradley household. After Madge's uncharacteristic weep when the miserable party had returned home on Saturday night, she had adopted an aloof attitude much more in keeping with her normal manner. Margaret had understandably withdrawn into herself, not wanting to discuss the events with either parents, the police or even Lizzie. Therefore when Madge insisted she return to work in the little gift shop on Burford High Street, she shut herself in her room to hide from the world, leaving Robert the job of apologizing to her employer for her absence, putting it down to a tummy bug or similar.

"Well, that's not going to solve anything." Madge was clearing the table as Robert got ready for work.

"Oh leave her alone, she'll come out when she's ready." He had had enough of recent happenings without her going on. Casting his gaze upwards he said quietly "She could do with a bit of understanding you know."
"And what am I supposed to do about that if she won't talk to me?"
"You're her mother."
"And just how do you think this is affecting me? I can't hold my head up when I go out."
Robert shook his head as his thoughts travelled to Beth. "I bet Lizzie's getting more attention" he mused.

The two police officers were comparing notes over a rather unappetizing cup of police tea. As they surveyed the reports spread in front of them, the younger one said "Can't see the Bradley chap involved myself. His account is identical to these other two, where there happened to be male drivers."
The more experienced one replied "Never be too sure. He could be involved in them all. But there were no stains on his clothing, and he was at home during one of the attacks, so it doesn't immediately point to him."
"There's one thing I don't understand." The sergeant scratched his chin.
"What's that?"
"We think the girls, and the men in each case, were hypnotized."
"Go on." The Det. Ch.Inspector smirked a little, guessing what was coming.
"So if whoever is practicing the art to get their way, well - what I'm getting at is why use the chloroform as well?"
"I've turned that one over." The senior man took another gulp of tea and grimaced. "You've got to remember, hypnotism is all very well if the subject is - how shall we say - suitable positioned. You couldn't just go up to someone in the street and put them under, or at least it's very unlikely."
"Ah," Sgt. Williams smiled. "You're saying it's a stand by, an 'if required' item."
"I'm not saying, I'm only making the suggestion."
The younger officer finished his tea, wiped his mouth and said "But somebody would have to have access to it wouldn't they?"

"True, we'll follow that one up."

Det. Ch.Insp.Jones sorted the papers into groups and beckoned, "Look at this."

The two heads bent over the table. The seemingly previously unconnected events were now forming into a pattern. Jones grabbed a map and thrust it toward Williams indicating him to get some coloured felt tip pens. "Let's see what this looks like." The sergeant grabbed the pens and spread the map in front of him. "Ready." he said.

"Right, these three were all found near Minster Lovell, all with male drivers, use one colour for that."

He waited for his assistant to make the marks.

"O.K. Now these two were both at the bottom of the hill leading down to Bourton, two women in the car each time." Another colour was marked.

"Now, we get to the bigger stuff. Six, no less and all near Leafield. These were all women driving alone. No chloroform used."

The sergeant leaned back viewing the spread, "At least that tells us something."

"It says a lot, but you've noticed there are different formats, which means we have at least three perpetrators."

The young man frowned. "But what if there are some that haven't been reported, for whatever reason."

"You mean somebody being where they shouldn't and not wanting to admit it. Well that's always a problem."

"So I've only really got the Minster Lovell lot and possibly the Bourton ones, as far as I know."

His superior hastened "Well, not there any more I should think, but they will move. These covens are very active, they will soon find another equally suitable place, it could be on your patch, or just outside. But I'd like you to keep involved. Your knowledge is useful."

Gathering up every paper, even the scraps used to make notes, the two men went their separate ways to work out a way to rid their county of this evil practice which was growing right under their noses.

The animosity between Zargot and Johhahn was growing rapidly. As far as the evil one was concerned, the underling had done his job and should now only been on hand as required or when summoned. The lesser entity, on the other hand, had no intention of relinquishing his hold on the J1 - J6 hybrids which he looked on as his.

The hybrids were being put through their paces, ready for Zargot's invasion of planet earth, and its one moon. He estimated that if he could throw the moon from the earth's gravity, it would probably cause enough chaos on the planet to draw attention from his intended attack on Saturn. Now that would really upset Jenny who had always found the utmost tranquility in the area.

He watched the latest ten craft go through their paces, each carrying two hybrids. It was not necessary to have any human form present; he could instruct the remaining brain cells left in the hybrids to perform any function just by using his thought patterns. Such was his extensive power. Just as he was about to select the next ten, which included J1-J6, he was surprised and annoyed when Johhahn's ideal appeared at his side.

"And who requested your presence?" The evil one's tone was cutting.

"I just wondered how things were going. Working with them so long, I naturally want to make sure there are no defects. Do you have a problem with that?"

The question was so direct it demanded a reply. Zargot paused. The thought that it may be better to have this troublemaker where he knew of his whereabouts may not be so bad after all.

"No" he replied cunningly. "In fact you are just in time for the next run. You may as well help."

Johhahn was wary but agreed. After all he was where he wanted to be by whatever means.

Zargot's order hit his mind. "Move the next six forward."

"Six!" The thought wave shot from Johhahn to his master. "You have been exercising ten up to now."

Zargot's smug aura extended to the other ideal. "Correct. But as you reminded me on earth, you have been improving as you went along. So. Let's see how much better this last bunch are." He paused. "Let's see if these six can do the work of ten." Johhahn knew he was being played with but he dare not show his hand, not yet.

Slowly, he moved his 'children' until they all hung just in front of Zargot. The eyes, which in all the other hybrids bore such a blank expression, now all focused on the subject before them. Even the evil one, with all his powers, was forced to feel the hatred emitting from the seven beings in his presence. Yes seven. For the concentration was coming from the creatures through Johhahn, and it was aimed at him.

Taking full charge of his own self, Zargot snapped "The others are returning. Get these to the launch area." And he immediately thought transported himself to receive his incoming servants.

"I'm sorry Lizzie; this is a terrible thing for you to come back to, with everything." Matron tried to console the sobbing girl.

"But she was nice." Lizzie was upset to hear of Mrs.Randle's departing, but the recent attack had left her low and she cried more than she would have in normal circumstances. Matron waited until she was a little more composed before she continued. "Unfortunately, the police want to speak to all the staff, and as many residents as possible."

"Why?" Lizzie didn't really want to see any more police just now.

"Oh I've already told them you were off sick, so they may not need you. It was Monday night you see."

"Oh." Then after a minute's pause, "how are the others taking it?"

"Not too badly really". Matron smiled. "She did keep to herself most of the time. I know you used to speak to her, but she was hardly aware of it." She tried to keep the girl's attention away from the matter in hand and for now she seemed to have succeeded, but she knew that questions would be asked later. Rising from her chair she said "Well there is plenty to do, best to keep busy."

"Yes, thank you matron."

"Oh and by the way, when you've finished the beds with the nurse, could you give Vernon a hand? I've asked him to tidy up the store room."

"Of course matron." Lizzie was always ready to help, and could often do the little simple jobs which gave the other staff time for more exacting work.

As she went into the day room, she spoke to the three female residents. "Hello ladies. Where are the men today?" The nearest to her said "Where do you think? In the usual place o'course." Lizzie glanced out of the windows in the conservatory to see Vernon holding court with

Pete and Old Joe in the greenhouse. They all appeared to be having a hearty laugh.

"Bet he's showing them mucky things," a disgruntled voice came across the room.

"What makes you say that Daisy?" Lizzie turned and patted the old lady's cushion. Normally the remark would have been comical, but today the girl couldn't see the humour in it.

"He shows them pictures of naked women. They've told me." The sentence was finished with a confirming nod.

"Oh well, never mind."

The nurse popped her head round the door. "Oh there you are, I'm starting the beds. Are you ready?"

Lizzie hurried from the room "Yes, I'm coming now."

CHAPTER 9

Detective Sergeant Williams was on the phone in his office to Detective Chief Inspector Jones.
"Well, that's even more interesting. (pause)Yes, that's the first time we've had the same m.o. in different places. How many reports did you say?"
The reply came down the line "Two out near Stratford, but identical to the Leafield ones. Look I'm just letting you know but we must meet again as soon as possible." They quickly arranged to meet that evening to discuss the latest developments. The problem was growing at too fast a pace. They had to do something soon before it got completely out of hand.
"Must go, there's someone to see me. See you tonight." Det. Sgt. Williams replaced the receiver and pulled together all the loose paper on his desk. He would like to have gone over the facts again, but there was urgency in the duty sergeant's voice, so he had better see the man waiting for him.

He got up, opened the door and was surprised to see his friend Barry Timms in the waiting area. "Oh, I thought it was a 'customer' " he laughed, but looking at the man's face, quickly guided him into his office, calling over his shoulder for a P.C to get him a cup of tea.
"Sit down old man. You look as if you'd seen a ghost."
"I wish that's all it was Roger. Sorry I know you're at work but I'm desperate." His friend was almost in tears.
"Well if I can help." The uniformed officer came in with two cups of tea, and they waited for him to depart before continuing.

The sergeant made a remark about the tea in a vain attempt to put his friend at ease, but realized he had got to gently draw out of him whatever had put him in this state.
"It's not Anne, or the children?"
"No - no - they're fine. At least at the moment. Oh God, Roger, she mustn't find out."

"Supposing you tell me everything. You know it's confidential. Just pour it out, any order, then we'll sort it out. It can't be that bad." He looked at Barry and indicated for him to start.

"I don't know where to begin; it's all such a mess. You see I was giving our neighbour a lift home." He looked under his lids knowing the reaction.

"You don't mean that good looking blond that's just moved in." Roger gave a man-to-man wink and nod.

"That one. Oh it wasn't planned you understand. No. I'd been over to see Fred Parsons, at Rissington, he's been very ill lately; anyway I was just getting in the car to go home, when there she is. Says she's been let down with a lift and could I help."

"Which of course you were only too happy to do." Roger was still trying to lighten the mood thinking it a bit of harmless fun. His smile fell as Barry continued.

"It never occurred to me what a coincidence it was that she was there at that precise time."

Roger leaned forward "You mean she planned it?"

"Oh I don't know. Well, we were travelling back, it was quite dark, and suddenly she asked me to stop." He paused, knowing the truth would seem a bit thin in the cold light of day.

"Did you think it strange?"

"Well no Roger, you see she said she felt a bit queasy, and I have to be honest with you, I thought she had probably had a drop to drink."

The sergeant offered, "And you didn't want her throwing up in your car eh?"

"Exactly. So I found a convenient place, a farmer's gateway, and stopped."

"Did she get out?"

Barry seemed a bit easier the more he could pour out without being criticized.

"That's the strange thing. I can't remember."

Roger looked serious. "Barry, this is important. What is the very last thing you do remember?"

His friend coughed. "I seem to remember her - um - well coming on to me" he looked embarrassed.

"Go on."

"Then - it's a blur, as though I'd been asleep and when I woke up --- "his voice trailed off but the sergeant waited until he was ready to continue, guessing this was getting to the important point. "I - I was, well - my trousers were undone and it was obvious I had just had sex with her. We were in the back seat. I was in a state I can tell you. She was putting her pants back on, and I came to as she was saying how good it had been, and how nobody must know."

Det.Sgt.Williams mused for a moment. This was a certainly a change of events, a woman this time. Barry looked at him. "You don't believe me do you?" His voice was weak from worry. "You know I'd never touch any other woman than Anne."

"Barry, I do believe you, and I'm very concerned at what has happened. You did right in coming to me. Look, maybe I shouldn't tell you this, but to put your mind at rest, you're not alone."

"What?" Barry's eyes were wide open now. "You mean she's going round doing, whatever it is, to others."

Roger held up his hand. "Please, you must keep that to yourself for now. Don't forget that all this conversation is in confidence."

"Oh yes, but -"

"Another thing," Roger was determined to put his friend's mind at ease in any way possible, "you don't know for sure that you did have sex with her."

Barry cut in "For God's sake man, I'd come off, I do know what it's like you know."

"Hang on a minute. Maybe you did. But it didn't have to be in her did it? She could have just wanted you to believe that." Barry sat back and said "Oh, I get what you mean. It was a con."

"I don't know, but it's a possibility. What I am saying is, don't take anything for granted until we can be sure, and above all don't mention it to Anne. You haven't have you?"

"No of course not. Why do you think I'm here?" After a second he said "What do you think happened Roger?"

"It's most likely you were put in some sort of trance."

"But why?"

Roger Williams gave another of his 'ask a stupid question' looks, to which his friend replied with an understanding "Oh."

Seeing his friend out with the promise to keep in touch, the sergeant wasted no time in picking up the phone to update his superior officer with this recent report.

Vernon Treloar, having finished his morning tasks was ready to undertake matron's request to tidy the storeroom.
"I've asked young Lizzie to give you a hand." She instructed him.
He smiled to himself. "Well of course you have, and I suppose you think it was all your idea." In a very self satisfied mood he made his way along the corridor.
"This should be very interesting," he thought as he unlocked the door. He had no sooner switched on the light and started to survey the accumulated stuff before him, than a voice behind him said "I've got to help you."

He turned slowly, half expecting a slight recognition on her face, but Lizzie was too wrapped in her own thoughts to give him much attention.
"Shall we start over here?" he indicated to a pile of linen, "perhaps it would give us more room if we closed the door."
She hesitated for a moment. He looked at her enquiringly. Was he familiar, even in his normal tousled rough and ready appearance? It gave him a sadistic thrill to think he could get this near and not have her suspect that this was the being who could possess her body at will.

But he was oblivious to the fact that any flashback Lizzie would receive, was not of him, but of Zargot's possession of him.

Now she was standing staring. "Door?" he repeated. She jumped.
"Oh yes, sorry. I was miles away."
"I could see that. Anything on your mind?"
"Well," she didn't want to explain about her attack, there wasn't much to say and she wouldn't have discussed it with him. But he had a kind look about him as he smiled sympathetically. Funny she hadn't noticed before.
She gave a little shrug and said "It's Gladys, sad isn't it, she seemed so alone. I hope I'm never alone like that."

"I'm sure you won't be." His voice was very lilting, very soothing. She felt secure with this older man.

"You're very kind Vernon." She looked up. He was standing very close to her now, and she quickly moved away.

"We must get on," she said as she started to grab at a pile of towels, her heart was beating as thought it wanted to escape. Why? Why did she feel like this? She had been drawn to this man with a desire never before experienced, as though he had something she craved, and yet not knowing what.

Smiling he replied "Yes, we'll have matron after us." He was satisfied with this little experiment. She had not recognized him and yet he knew she wanted him, and although he could have taken her there and then, he was too cautious, too well practiced in the art to be so careless. Those kinds of activities must take place well away from work where he could be traced. She was in his grasp, she was his.

The news of the ever increasing evil spreading over the earth was being carefully monitored by the spirals on Eden. Jenny was for ever alert awaiting Zargot's moves, but she was equally aware that he would jump on any opportunity afforded him by lesser entities such as the Vexons. Covens of witches seemed to be springing up like weeds, although some mortals merely joined because it seemed to be the thing of the moment, and they soon left when meetings got a little spooky.

The more serious among them tried their hand at rituals, attempting to call up the evil ones, and wallowing in sex orgies with willing parties. The watching entities revelled in the naivety of these amateurs, but used the chance to gain a foothold by opening a small portal for future use. There will always be the Gladys Randles ready to meddle.

The Vexons by comparison used their hypnotic powers to overcome the victims, who, had they retained their full senses would never have succumbed to the disgusting sexual acts expected of them. This made it all the more stimulating as the insatiable pleasure came with the taking over and possessing of a person, male or female, but not having it given willingly.

Graham had returned from a sweep of southern England to report a surge of ritual slayings, mainly animals, but in one location, a newly born baby. This terrible development triggered a shock wave through the spirals on Eden, and a plan was put into operation to fight this phase as a priority operation.

Madge was getting ready to go out. Her husband was still not sure where she had been popping off to recently. "Some women's meeting" was all he could get out of her.

"Do you really have to go tonight Madge?"

"And why shouldn't I? You are going out, what's the difference may I ask?" She carried on getting herself ready, trying to ignore his questions.

He sighed. "You know I always see Jack on Thursdays, have done for years."

"So?" she shrugged.

"But you were out the other night, and you didn't say where."

She turned on him. "So, it's come to this has it? I have to fill in a log book of my whereabouts."

"No, No, don't be stupid, I was thinking of Margaret being on her own, that's all. I don't suppose you gave her a moment's consideration."

"Look Robert, if that girl insists on locking herself away every moment, that's her business. You can't help people who won't be helped." She turned to make up her face.

"Well, I'm going to give young Lizzie a ring, see if she'd come over for a while."

Madge grabbed her bag and coat. "Well we all know what you are ringing her for don't we? I'm sure Beth will be only too pleased to chat to you." With that she left with a flourish that left the air trembling behind her.

Robert sat down, his emotions a mixture of anger almost verging on hatred for his wife, and worry about his daughter. He picked up the 'phone and dialled Beth's number. She answered almost immediately.

"Robert, this is a nice surprise."

"Well actually, I wanted a favour."

"Of course, what's the matter?"

He explained about Margaret's change in behaviour since the attack, and wondered if Lizzie would like to go over. Beth suggested dropping Margaret off with them but as Robert explained, it wasn't an easy task getting her out of her room. Neither of them was sure if his daughter would even let Lizzie into her sanctuary in case her very presence triggered off memories of that awful night. Beth couldn't help but wonder if the mother's treatment was making the girl worse. "Not much love shown there," she thought.

Lizzie looked up expectantly, and as her mother related the conversation, she nodded eagerly, always anxious to help. They decided to give it a try and Robert agreed to pick Lizzie up straight away. Beth blushed a little at the thought of seeing him, even for a moment, but quickly put such thoughts from her mind as she awaited his arrival.

CHAPTER 10

Maybe if Robert had known of his wife's intentions for that evening, his anger would have turned to fear.

She had only just left the house, when a car containing three women pulled up alongside and she quickly got in. The driver would have been instantly recognizable to Barry Timms as the blond passenger he had described to his friend. They all travelled in silence for a while, then Deana, the front passenger announced without turning round, "It's the same place tonight." Zena, the woman sitting with Madge in the back seat leaned over and whispered "It's your big night. Time to prove yourself." The voice was not informing, it was threatening, saying "perform to satisfaction, or else." Madge nodded in the darkness. She felt a thrill at this new experience, but a deep rooted fear that she couldn't handle what was expected of her.

They had left Burford and were heading out into the country, past a few lonely farms, until they suddenly turned off the road and were bumping down a dirt track to a nearby spinney. It was only about two hundred yards, but felt like miles as they bounced around hitting unseen potholes. They rounded a corner and were immediately out of sight of the road.

"Out" the order came from Mandy, the driver, and followed by a strong shove from Madge's back seat companion.

They all got out quietly in the dark and moved to the back of the car. Mandy opened the boot, and the small interior light gave them enough illumination to change their outfits. Madge had previously been told exactly what she must do, and now she donned a short tight dress, black tights and high heeled shoes, finishing the whole look with a long blond wig. The other three all dressed in black leather, soon merged with the darkness. They gathered up the tools of their trade, left their own belongings in the boot and prepared for the night's evil deeds.

Deana, now gripping a small torch, led the way into the dense spinney until they reached their ritual ground. As Zena took her place at the altar, the others lit spicy scented candles in a circle in front of it. The high priestess, as she liked to be known was a tall woman, but here in the flickering shadows, took on even greater dimensions. She seemed to grow in front of them, and her slow chanting began to fill their bodies until the heady atmosphere began to dull their senses.

Madge had been nervous when she had been told she would attract the prey for the night, and had been a little concerned as to how she would get back to the road in the shoes she now wore. Also the road was very lonely. What if no one came along there? Unless of course, Zena had arranged it.

Zena, like Vedron, was a Vexon, lusting after the physical enjoyments, possessing, insanely jealous, and a lesbian. The others were merely her followers. They helped her get what she wanted, but there was no danger of them taking her spoils, for they were straight women, and didn't want any of her catches. They only wanted the male conquests, which, with a little training she had taught them to acquire, thus keeping them happy, and safeguarding her own little toys.

This was how Mandy had savoured the delights of Barry Timms. Oh, she had had him alright, in every way possible. And she wanted him again, but he would probably be on his guard, not knowing exactly what had happened, so she would have to use other means next time.

As Zena afforded her girls so much pleasure, they were only too happy to repay her by assisting her in her own desires, added to the fact they were semi hypnotized, and partly drugged by the candles.

"Now." She called as she lifted her arms. A sudden chill flowed over the clearing making the candles flicker. It was early autumn but this had nothing to do with the atmospheric conditions, this was the sign of approaching evil, summoned by the high priestess.

Deana and Mandy stood either side of Madge, hardly recognizable as the heartless mother of Margaret who had recently stood in a similar position but surrounded by men. They were now in the centre of the circle. Slowly, Zena came, almost floating from the altar and stood in the circle facing them.

Madge's brain was trying to piece everything together. She wondered why she had not been sent to the road yet to trap a lone male driver into helping her, then enticing him for their delights. She felt dizzy, not liking the way this was going, but unable to respond as she was held on either side as Zena, staring straight into her eyes came nearer and nearer.

A pale green mist rose around the Vexon as she drank in the sight of the female, trembling like a lamb about to be sacrificed. With a slow wave to each sentinel, Madge's clothes were gradually removed. Again the victim wanted to protest but something powerful told her this was useless. She now stood in only her high heeled shoes and blond wig as the mist enveloped her and she sank into blackness.

Zargot had dispatched his first assignment, not to earth as was expected, but to the area around Saturn. Nothing was done to hide the attack and the zombies and their crafts were soon destroyed by the local defense inhabitants. It had been Zargot's intention to send J1-J6 on this little escapade, but Johhahn had intervened much to the evil one's annoyance.

The news quickly reached the spirals on Eden, and after the first stab of confusion as to his methods, it was realized he was attempting to create a diversion from his objective. The ultimates would therefore not be drawn away, giving him a clear run to earth.

Jenny was secretly glad that at least some of the creatures would now, hopefully, be at peace and a prayer for them rippled through the spirals. Marie and Graham were dispatched to be on hand in case of any transitions, should the ideals have been trapped in the forms. This would also tell them much of the general state of the others, and preparations could be made for them all to be received on their passing, which could not be soon enough.

As suspected, the Schynings were only too ready to help disrupt and destroy the crafts' electrical power, even if it meant a slow end for the occupants. As many manned light spheres and panels that could be mustered were on stand by awaiting the order to attack. They were positioned at strategic electrical points, so as to be on full power at any time.

Jenny knew the reason for this little show of strength. The evil one, who had been planning revenge, was about to put it into operation.

The questions to be answered were when, where, and exactly how? Soon she would have the answers.

"Hello. It's me, Lizzie." Silence came from Margaret's room, so the visitor tapped again. The door opened a crack to reveal a pale dishevelled girl, obviously in desperate need of attention. Robert drew his breath in sharply, shocked at the sight, but relieved that the girl had appeared.

"Are you alone?" The question was barely audible.

"Yes, well, your dad's here, but he's going out, so I've come to see you. We could have a chat, or just sit if you'd rather."

Margaret tried to peer round the door. "Is she out then?"

Robert leaned forward, "Yes love, she's gone to that meeting she goes to, don't know when she'll be back."

The door opened further. "Alright."

Robert didn't want to make her retreat again, having come this far, so he moved back as he said "Perhaps you could make Lizzie a drink, " but looking at the weak state of her said "or Lizzie, if you want to do it, everything's in the kitchen, just help yourself."

"Thank you Mr. Bradley. We'll be fine, won't we Margaret?" The other girl barely nodded. Lizzie couldn't help but compare her to the old folks she tended at work. At least it was good experience, and she didn't flinch at the slightest unpleasantness.

Although she wasn't the brightest, Lizzie realized she had to get some fluids, and later nourishment down her friend. Then perhaps she could find some way to get her to have a wash. Margaret couldn't have been in kinder hands.

Robert left with the promise of not being too late, but wondering if he should have stayed. "No." he told himself, “she's better with young Lizzie, and maybe she'll do her good."

Margaret was slumped in an easy chair, and Lizzie, as she went to make herself comfortable on the settee said "I wouldn't mind a drink myself. Have one with me?" The reply was a nod, but even that was encouraging, so Lizzie went into the kitchen humming softly. When she returned she was carrying a tray with two cups of tea and a plate of biscuits. She had the sense not to try and get her friend to have too much at first, and if she could get her to have a drink and even one biscuit, that would be a start.

She would have preferred to suggest she fetch a doctor, but knew at this stage, Margaret would just pull away. One step at a time would have to suffice. Handing Margaret her tea she said "I've haven't half missed you." Her friend sipped the drink and immediately heaved. "Steady on "Lizzie was at her side "take it easy, no rush." She purposely didn't stare or appear to take much notice of the physical appearance, and sat down with her tea, making small talk. Her friend stared ahead, her eyes brimming with sadness and despair.

"Have a bikkie." Lizzie picked up a digestive and put it into Margaret's hand. "'Scuse fingers, they are clean," and she gave one of her infectious little laughs that made the other girl look up with the suggestion of a smile.

With no pressure on her, Margaret eventually started to come out of herself. Slowly at first, until she was holding her first conversation for days, although there would be a pause as she cried from time to time.

"She blames me you see." Her head shook almost in disbelief.

Lizzie was indignant, thinking of Beth's attitude to the matter.

"But how can she? It wasn't our fault. We don't even remember. We aren't sure are we?"

"She says I'm a dirty little slut, and not fit to be called her daughter." At this outpouring, Margaret sobbed bitterly. The two held each other, hugging for comfort and reassurance. After a few moments Lizzie said "I know, why don't you come and stay with me for a while, I'm sure Mum wouldn't mind, we'd look after you."

"I couldn't."

"Why not?" Lizzie held her at arms length, nearly shaking her by the shoulders, but looking at the dejected figure realized she must be very gently with her. She had gained her trust, and she didn't want to loose it at this vital stage. Margaret just shook her head.

"I'm ringing her now," Lizzie was in charge and nothing was going to stop her helping this girl back to her normal state. She crossed to the 'phone and dialled her home number.

"Hello." Beth answered quickly.

"Mum it's me. Can Margaret come and stay with us, she needs help, she can have my room, and ----"

"Just a minute, slow down. Now. Tell me slowly."

Her daughter explained the girl's physical and mental state and begged to let her mother help her.

"I'd love nothing better my dear, but what about her parents. We can't just up and bring her away against their will."

"Mum, she's eighteen." The pleading coming down the phone line touched Beth. She was a kindly woman, and would have helped any soul in trouble, and now she felt she could help this poor thing especially as the mother obviously had no interest.

"Look. I'll tell you what we'll do," her brain was racing to find the right answer, "Robert, I mean Margaret's father will be back soon. Get him to ring me as soon as he comes in, and we'll see. No promises mind."

"Oh Mum you are an angel." The phone was put down, leaving Beth looking at the receiver.

She smiled and made her way upstairs to the tiny spare bedroom collecting clean linen from the airing cupboard on the way. As she quickly made up the bed she thought "Can't blame the girl, she must take after me." She hoped desperately that Robert would bring both girls to her before Madge had chance to intervene, then she could give the Margaret the sort of treatment she should have received all along.

Less than an hour had elapsed when Beth heard a car pull up and stop. Jumping up she ran to the window to see Robert and Lizzie almost carrying Margaret to the house. She opened the front door for them to come straight in.

"Oh I'm so glad you've brought her" she said to Robert, but on seeing the state of his daughter in the light she gave a little gasp and beckoned for them to put her on the settee. Automatically she put her arms protectively round her and whispered "You'll be alright now."

Turning to look up at Robert she said "I hope you don't think we're interferring, but Lizzie was ----"

His hand went up to silence her "Beth, you don't know how grateful I am to you for getting her out of there" he put his hand on Lizzie's shoulder, "and you Lizzie, you've done wonders, thank you so much."

As he turned back to Beth she noticed his eyes were full of tears. "I didn't stop to ring; I didn't want to waste any more time." Beth got up and moved with him to the door leaving Lizzie to sit with her friend. Robert stopped with his hand on the doorknob, "I'll see you alright for money for her food etc."

"Oh don't be silly" Beth started to argue but he was insistent.

"After all that you are doing for us. Please, leave it to me."

"If it will make you happy," she realized as the words left her mouth, and by the look on his face that she could make him happier that the woman he had married. Quickly she added "How will you explain it to Madge?"

"I'll tell her Margaret wanted to stay with Lizzie. But to be honest I don't think she'll care that much. That's the trouble you see, only thinks of herself."

They were out of sight of the girls, and he leaned forward and gave her a gently kiss on the cheek. Her lips parted and her hand went to the spot he had just touched. She squeezed his hand and watched him go, her stomach knotted with a thrill she knew she could not control.

With every ounce of will power, she pulled herself together and returned to the living room. "Right ladies. I've put you in the room next to Lizzie, Margaret. If you leave your doors ajar you can chat to each other."

To Beth's surprise it was Margaret who spoke. "It's very kind of you Mrs. Stokes, to take me in like this."

"Oh think nothing of it my dear. Now Lizzie, why don't you take Margaret upstairs and show her where everything is in the bathroom and you can lend her one of your nighties for now." She hoped that even a little wash at this point might coax the self esteem back.

Secretly she wondered how the girl was going to negotiate the stairs, but with Lizzie's help she seemed to be doing just fine. Beth flopped down in the chair and mischievously wondered just what Madge's reaction would be when she returned that evening.

CHAPTER 11

Detective Chief Inspector Jones was visiting Detective Sergeant Williams to recap on recent events. It was almost three weeks since they had started the colour co-ordinated map showing all the recent reports of hypnotized sexual attacks, and certain areas were somewhat overcrowded. There had been a marked increase in the number of female attackers, and although the public had been warned of the activity in an attempt to curb it, there were still reports flooding in.

"By the way," the senior man was sorting through a file, "one of our lads has mentioned this in passing."

Det. Sgt. Williams leaned over to see what was being indicated." Oh, we've had one of those."

"Yes I thought you'd recognize the signs."

The sergeant thought for a minute, "What was her name, lived at the nursing home, I know Mrs. Randle, Gladys Randle. Doctor thought she had been strangled at the time but it came out as natural causes. That's right; she had bruises on her neck."

"Look at these then." Jones shoved a handful of reports towards him.

After a couple of minutes perusal, the sergeant said "Bit of a bloody coincidence."

"I thought you'd find that interesting. Six reports no less. All bruised necks. All natural causes verdict. One was even found with their hands still round their own neck."

"Oh come on," Det. Sgt Williams exclaimed." Somebody placed them there afterwards. This is a cover up surely?"

"All in different locations, different doctors. We can't prove anything, at the moment."

"You couldn't do it." The sergeant was musing.

"Strangle yourself? You wouldn't think so. The grip would relax as the person became unconscious."

"Just a minute. Why are you mentioning this now? “Then after a pause "You think there is a connection don't you?"
The Det. Ch. Insp. was smiling. "I certainly think we should keep it at the back of our minds, with all that's going on don't you?"
"Hmm. Perhaps the killer doesn't have to be there you mean," jokingly adding "uses remote control eh?"
"Who knows?"
"You aren't serious." But looking at Jones' face said "You are."
The older man gathered the reports together saying "Like I said, who knows, yet?"

Vernon was listening intently as Lizzie happily chatted to Old Joe, telling him about having her friend to stay, and what good fun they were having. The Vexon was frustrated. He needed Lizzie and was determined to find a way to have her again, as soon as possible.
"And my mum's going out tonight, old Mrs. Spence is poorly again, and mum's going to take her some home made jam." Vernon moved nearer. Old Joe cupped his hand to his ear to listen, nodding. "Ah your ma's a good woman lass; you won't go far wrong if you follow in her footsteps."

So. Beth would be out and the two girls alone. But how long had he got? It didn't matter, he had ways of stretching the time to give him all he needed. Tonight then. He could possess her body again, for she was his.

If Robert had been worried about his wife's reaction when he had moved Margaret to Beth's, he need not have been, for she returned home apparently drunk although not smelling of alcohol, and went straight to bed. Since then she had gone out almost every other night, making various excuses, none of which her husband believed. His attentions were drawn towards his daughters' rapid recovery and above all his beloved Beth.

His wife seemed to have no interest in her daughter whatsoever, and strangely enough, although he wasn't complaining, no interest in him. He fully expected a roasting for visiting Beth's house so often, for whatever reason, but none came. He did not press Madge for details of her activities, for he no longer loved her, and since her treatment of Margaret, he actually loathed the woman.

It never occurred to him that she could be taking part in the kind of ritual to which the girls had been subjected, except that she herself was the prey, Zena's plaything and object of lust.

Madge didn't even know why she kept going back, she remembered little of any night's proceedings, except for the fact that she felt she was trapped and had no will of her own. She seemed to come back to reality in a state of ecstasy and fulfillment, which fuelled her need for more, so she returned again and again.

One chilly night, she was picked up as usual and driven to the hunting ground. Something in the air was different; all four females could feel it. Zena was exhilarated, expectant that something big was going to happen, but the others were very apprehensive, shivering in the constant cold draughts which were filling the clearing.

Quickly and rather nervously the three lit the candles, partly for light but also hoping to gain a little warmth. The high priestess appeared oblivious of their discomfort and stood at her altar, arms raised, already beginning her chant. But she was being observed.

The success of her hold over these mortals was no accident, but carefully engineered by greater powers, and now by Zargot himself, for, although she did not realize it, she was his tool, his implement, his evil wand. Zena revelled in the fact that the power was her own, for was she not a Vexon and above the lower earthly beings. Such was her folly.

Zargot now hovered unseen over the gathering, flitting, touching, and making his presence felt through the females. Again the three shifted uneasily while the high priestess chanted in words never before heard by them.

Madge was still fully dressed when the column of green mist rose from the altar, then slowly spread over the circle. In its depth the women could make out a hideous horned image, part man, part animal resembling a wolf. But it kept changing and growing until it swamped them and swirled around the circle like a tornado. Although Zena appeared in a deep trance, the rest were not hypnotized and were surrounded by sheer terror. They all tried to scream, but it choked in their throats. Desperately they tried to cling to each other, but in the mist now mingled with the candle smoke, none could find a companion for support and all frantically grasped at the night air until suddenly they all fell together, unconscious.

Zargot entered Zena's body as she selected her prey, stripped her completely and ravaged her body in a way no decent being would accept. Delighted at the progress of this small cult, the evil one left the group for his next objective, Vedron.

Jenny was communicating with the other ultimate beings on Eden. She was well aware of the growing covens in all parts of the earth, and although her intervening had slowed the evil march a little, she knew it was insufficient as a long term project. On her command, smaller portals were being closed almost as soon as they were opened, but immediately replaced by a new opening.

Also, the worry uppermost in her mind was why Zargot had not started his invasion. She felt he was playing with her. Attracting her or her ultimates to the spreading evil, and waiting to make his attack at just the right moment. Many times she had tried momentarily to get into his ideal but his power equalled hers and she was unsuccessful, feeling like the mouse being toyed with by the cat.

Her thought reached Marie who had been carefully monitoring Lizzie and Margaret. "You did well to maneouver her out of the way Marie; she is making good progress now." It had been Jenny's idea to get Margaret safely planted at Beth's and she was pleased how smoothly the operation had gone.

Marie projected "Yes, Margaret is really happy where she is. Can we leave her there for now?"

"In the circumstances, until we see the outcome of her mother." Jenny had been observing Madge's recent activities.

Graham was included in this conference and contributed for the first time. "If it isn't indelicate, I find Robert is more than pleased at the placing."

Jenny intervened, "The romantic as ever Graham. Well we shall see."

As she closed the conference, she dispatched Matthew to view Vendron's whereabouts, and sent the ultimate at the top of the upper spiral to view Madge, knowing greater power would be needed if Zargot or one of his crew had been involved.

Johhahn had seemingly recovered from his horrific transition from Earth to Zargon, but the evil entities continued to fire the tormenting jibes not willing to let the matter rest. One not so strong willed as he would have crumbled under the mental pressure, but Johhahn, assured in the knowledge he held a deadly weapon, paid them little heed.

He regularly visited the holding station, especially when Zargot was occupied elsewhere, and carefully monitored and re-monitored his beloved J1 - J6 hybrids, his children. His main concern was not to let them be dispatched until he was ready. Zargot had already tried this on the dummy run, but his own intervention had thwarted it, making him realize that he must be diligent at all times. It was obvious that the evil one suspected him but to what extent he could only guess. Therefore he must not slip his guard for an instant.

He was continually changing the position of the six, hoping for their anonymity but he now had a problem. While the remainder still hung zombie fashion, being recharged at regular intervals, the J1 - J6 hybrids were becoming noticeably different. Not only were their eyes seeing all before them, they were taking on a compelling look which held anyone in their path.

Even Johhahn now stood rooted to the spot as he went to check them. Using all his power he wrenched his mind to take charge of the moment. He felt the power of these six taking him over, but that was not the plan. He was supposed to control them until they all acted as one, on his command only.

He stared at J1, the nearest to him. The eyes seemed bigger than before. Whereas the other hundreds of specimens had mere slits, this baby had wide openings. On programming he was aware he had made his special six larger than the others, but never like this. A slight apprehension ran through his ideal as he surveyed the other five. They were all the same.

The hybrids were hung in formation, one behind the other, so that each one faced the back of the one in front. Therefore to view the faces of all six, Johhahn would stand facing J1 and look down the line. It was impossible to see the complete faces of all of them, due the close positioning, but this time Johhahn felt he was being observed by all of them. He even imagined seeing them all full face, staring, willing, hypnotic.

He tried to take control, but the power radiating from the six was almost overpowering. Also he noticed the ones in front and behind them were draining. The J hybrids were pulling the power for themselves.

With every ounce of his spiral power he wrenched free from the grip and in panic turned his attention to the weakening neighbours. If this continued to happen, Zargot's wrath would be unequalled, and Johhahn knew for sure that he would be forced to exist in a mental hell for eternity.

With slight relief, he noticed the other hybrids returning to power. They were all programmed to boost themselves when the impulses reached a certain level, but if the J's were draining them to such an extent, it was possible they could override the command.

Johhahn was therefore a little uneasy as he returned to Zargon to the usual evil waves which always greeted him.

Ignoring them he enquired through the lower spiral as to Zargot's whereabouts. Getting no sensible reply he enquired from above, from the upper spiral, but was informed in no uncertain terms, that it was of no concern of his. He sent a self satisfied ripple through the lower level, but his inner feeling was far from calm.

Before he sought out Vedron, Zargot decided to take a quick thought travel to the holding station. He didn't trust the lower level one, and made continual visits hoping to catch him out. He arrived, assumed no form and quickly observed the creatures. All appeared well. Had he taken a closer look at the J's, he would have seen the eyes as programmed, not the wide open format which had secretly terrified their part creator earlier.

Satisfied he returned to England, Earth, and waited for his next moment of pleasure.

CHAPTER 12

Vedron was preparing himself, preening and admiring his physique in front of his mirror. He went through quite a long process to get ready for any ritual, the anticipation all being part of his enjoyment.

Tonight would test his powers to the full, for not only was he working alone, but in an unprepared place. He was aware of the good aura surrounding Beth, her daughter and her house. And now Margaret was living there, even temporarily, would make his job that little more difficult.

There was also the chance that another spell of his hypnotism might just trigger a memory in one or both of the young ladies. But his sexual urge took over all logic and drove him to take the chance in order to achieve his sexual fulfillment. After all he was a Vexon, and such was their way of existence, often creating their own destruction.

He left his house and walked to within a few yards of Beth's, lurking in the shadows until he saw her leave clutching her little pot of jam. In case she returned unexpectedly for any reason, he waited a few more minutes before making his way to the door.

Very conveniently, the entrance door was at the back of the cottage, out of sight from general passers by. A narrow lane led from the road, and was only used by people who lived in, or visited the few cottages it serviced.

In a few quick strides, Vedron had slipped up the lane, rounded the corner of the building, and now stood at the door. A long dark coat covered his black outfit, and a cap pulled well down hid most of his face. Although it was dark, he knew the moment the door opened he would be flooded in light, so having tapped gently; he stood back almost at the lane.

Lizzie and Margaret looked at each other.

"Who on earth can that be?" Lizzie looked bewildered at the door. "Better go and see who it is." As she got up, her friend joined her, so they were together as Lizzie called, with the door still closed, "Who's there?"
"I'm looking for Mrs. ---" the last word was muffled.
Shrugging, Lizzie gingerly opened the door and looked at nothing but the night. Vedron was still standing out of the glare and said in a very soft muted voice, "Is this right for Mrs. Smith?"
A little relieved Lizzie said "Oh no, she's the next one up the lane, you can't miss it."

Slowly Vedron began his hypnotizing chant until he had moved to the doorway and was facing the two girls. When he was sure they would obey him, he quickly stepped inside and closed the door behind him. He ordered them to both sit on the settee. Lizzie quickly responded but Margaret was very slow to succumb, a slight look of horrific recognition covering her features.

As they awaited his next command, he quickly checked that the door was locked, and then inspected the windows to see that all the curtains were drawn. He moved in front of Margaret who was slumped on the settee, a far away look on her face, and told her to remain there until he instructed her further. Now he could turn his attentions to the purpose of his visit.

As he spoke in his lilting tones, he drew Lizzie to her feet and led her behind the settee. There, he told her to undress and lay on the floor, which she did obediently. Within seconds, he stood above her, himself completely naked, then lowered himself to her and frantically released his pent up frustration. This was merely a starter and in no way enough to satisfy the sex fiend. He grabbed Lizzie's hand and ordered her to stimulate him again, which she obligingly did. From this moment on, the thrill that surged through Vedron's body was unsurpassed, reaching newly found heights.

Afterwards, he ordered her to dress and sit beside her friend. Once again he stood before them telling them to wake in five minutes, and remember nothing of what had taken place since Beth left. With that he unlocked the door and slipped away into the darkness.

Zargot, although grateful to the Vexons for supplying him with such an evening's pleasure, despised them for being mere putty in his hands. They rarely guessed he was sharing what they considered to be their enjoyment, believing it to be all their own doing.

But now it was time to inspect the hybrids and he was instantly at the holding zone. Automatically he sought out the J group. He knew something was going on here, but the only way to find out was to hold back and observe.

It was clear that Johhahn would not be forthcoming, but the being was plotting something.

Zargot had not taken on any apparent form, feeling it unnecessary. After all, there was only him and the hybrids. On finding the J batch he paused, or to be absolutely correct, he was paused. Taken by surprise, he did not have time to react to protect himself as he felt the power from the six crushing his ideal from all sides. As he used all his power to fight back he was transported at speed up and down the rows, his ideal going through each hybrid until he was back in his original position, and free.

He looked closely at the six one at a time, but they had all taken on the same blank expressions of their companions.

Knowing he had to act quickly before things got out of hand, he thought travelled back to Zargon and took his place at the head of the upper spiral to contemplate.

Five minutes to the second after Vedron had departed, Lizzie and Margaret awoke. It took a few moments for Lizzie to realize something was wrong and she dashed to the bathroom to examine herself. Margaret staggered after her, very dazed, thinking she had been in a proper sleep.

"What's the matter Liz?" A muffled voice called through the closed door. Her friend was almost crying. "I - I - I'm not sure." She was cleaning herself from the remains of Vedron's attack, and putting her panties into the washing basket.

It suddenly occurred to her, that if something had happened, and she felt sure it must have, to tell Margaret could be undoing all the good achieved to date.

"I'll be down in a minute, um, thought I'd started."

"Oh O.K. Shall I put the kettle on?"

"Please." As soon as the other girl had gone, she went to her room and rummaged in the undie drawer for clean knickers. Putting them on, she sat on the bed, her brain trying to piece together what had happened. But all she could remember was her mother leaving, and then her waking up in this mess.

Although she wasn't over bright, Lizzie knew that this was important enough to tell her mother about on her return, but having her friend's welfare at heart; she knew she must keep it out of her hearing at all costs.

Margaret seemed none the worse for wear, but she had only been put in a trance and not raped, so no damage appeared to have been done for now. She came from the kitchen with two mugs of tea and when Lizzie joined her, the two sat watching the television until Beth came back.

Robert looked up from his book as his wife almost staggered in and made her way to the stairs without giving him a glance.

"Just one moment there madam." His voice was cutting. She paused for a second but then continued to try and clamber up the first step.

"I said, just a moment." As he moved nearer the full extent of her dishevelled appearance hit him.

"What in God's name woman----?" he started to ask, but she cut in "Oh I doubt God had much to do with it."

He very roughly manhandled her upstairs and almost threw her on the bed. In the full light, he saw just what a disgusting mess she was.

"You've been attacked. Why didn't you say?"

"Oh shut up stupid man, I haven't been attacked."

"Then would you mind telling me just how you got into this state?" Then very piercingly "In words you think I might just be able to understand."

"You know nothing." She spat the words in his face.

"Then I shall call the police." So saying he made to leave the room but she clawed the air to stop him.

"No. No. Not the police."

"Oh?" he replied sarcastically. "Now we are getting somewhere."

She eyed him suspiciously in silence.

His face darkened. "Ah. So that's it. You've got a lover. Another man. And he's given you what for." Satisfied he said "I'm right aren't I?"

Reluctantly she sighed. "If you say so."
"Well either that or you're on the game. Is that it, you dirty little trollop?"
"Think what you will."
He looked at her in utter disgust. "No wonder you're such a poor mother to Margaret." Leaving her alone he said "You make me sick."

He had recently been sleeping in the spare room and now was glad he wouldn't have to share a bed with such a creature.

Margaret had now returned to work after her period of 'illness' as it was called. Beth was only too pleased to keep her living under her roof, and she and Robert came to an agreement over payment.

On the morning after the recent episode, she sent the two girls off to their respective jobs and immediately picked up the 'phone to the police. Lizzie had managed to give her as many details as she could, and Beth wanted to pass on the information at her earliest chance, without arousing Margaret's suspicion. She realized the police would want to see Lizzie but that would have to wait for now as she wanted to keep everything as calm as possible in her household. If Madge didn't show any interest in her daughter's welfare, then she would.

Within an hour, Det.Sgt Williams was knocking on the door. He entered quickly on her invitation, scanned the room and beckoned her to sit down.

Briefly he outlined his connection with the recent happenings including the girls' rapes, explaining that they were trying to keep all the relevant details confined to the officers involved.
"My Chief's on the way, but he wanted me to find out all I could in the meantime." he began.
"Would you like some tea, it wouldn't take a minute?" Beth went to get up.
"No, No, thank you all the same. I'd like to get on if that's alright?"
"Oh of course."
The sergeant took a breath. "This could be the break we've been looking for, an actual site where something took place."
Beth said "But we don't know for sure do we?"
"That's where I need your help."
"My help. But I was out. I went to Mrs. Spence's, she's poorly you see."

"Yes, I'm aware of that. What I'm saying is" he paused for a moment "look Mrs. Stokes, I realize this isn't nice for you, but there are certain things I need to see."

"Oh? Such as? I mean, I only want to help."

"I know you do and I'll make it as acceptable as possible." He looked at her, gave a reassuring little smile and nodded invoking her agreement. When he was sure he had reached the right moment, he said "You haven't washed any of her clothes yet have you?"

"Well no, I was going to, but then I thought," her eyes dropped, "I did wonder if you would need to see them for those tests you do." She wasn't finding it easy to discuss her daughter's soiled underwear with a man, police officer or not. With relief he said "Oh good."

He opened his case and took out labelled bags. "Could you take me to where the garments are?" As he followed her up the stairs she said "I think there's only her pants, you have to take them away don't you?" The thought flashed through his mind that it would be difficult to examine them here, but he made allowances for the woman's distress.

They reached the bathroom and Beth pointed to the basket. "They are on the top." The sergeant put on plastic gloves and carefully lifted the soiled garment, marking the label with all the details.

They went back down stairs and he carefully put the bag into his case.

"The next think I want to do is go over your house." He was being very gentle, knowing that, to achieve his results he needed her full co-operation.

"What for?" she didn't want to object, but her mind couldn't fathom any reason for examining her house.

A sharp knock at the door made her jump.

"That'll be the Chief, I expect" Det.Sgt Williams was already on his feet and making his way to the door. As the senior man entered, his colleague introduced him to Beth and added, "This lady is being extremely helpful.

Det.Ch.Insp. Jones looked at Beth and said "We do appreciate this. Has the sergeant explained what we have to do?"

"Well he has Lizzie's pants. Is there more? I've told him all she told me."

The Chief smiled. "I'm afraid there is. What we need to do is to go over your house. You see we don't know where it happened, assuming something did of course."
"But---" Beth tried to speak.
"You say your daughter can't remember anything?"
"That's right."
"Well, we will have to speak to her, but for now we may just find something to help us. Can I ask, have you cleaned this morning?"
"No, I was going to, but after I'd 'phoned and they said to leave everything, I thought I'd better do as they said."
"Quite right." Jones looked around the downstairs room. He could do with getting the woman out of the way so he said, "Any chance of a cup of tea my dear?"
Beth was only too pleased to be able to be hospitable and she quickly went to the kitchen. "You too sergeant, do you fancy one now?"
"Oh yes, that would be nice," he nodded.

As soon as she was out of earshot, the two men whispered quickly.
"I suppose the place has been well trampled over already," Jones began.
"I've not seen anything obvious, but I suppose that's only to be expected. Hardly going to leave anything in full view." Williams cast his eyes around the immediate area.
"Oh well, may as well start here" the Chief said "Then we'll move upstairs." He went to the kitchen and peered round the door. "Sorry to ask this Mrs. Stokes, but could you remain in here for just a minute. Give us a bit more room."
Reluctantly she said "Oh, well alright then."

Left alone they examined the chairs, settee, cushions and all soft furnishings for any marks or traces of clothing fibres, hairs etc.
"Nothing yet." the younger man shrugged. "He probably took her upstairs.
"Or she went willingly." The Det.Ch.Insp. was still not one hundred percent sure that the girl had not invited a boyfriend in, gone too far, then panicked as was so often the case. It was only the fact of the spate of events that made him pursue this one. Added to which there was no evidence of such from the girl's friend, but he only had the woman's word for that. She had begged that Margaret not be questioned at this

point and he had agreed for the time being, but with no long lasting promise. It may prove essential.

However, for now he was content to be able to examine a possible scene. Another strange thing shot across his mind. Of all the happenings, this was the first one reportedly taking place in someone's home. Again the nagging suspicion took over. Was the girl merely using the previous attack, whether true or not, to cover up her goings on now?

"What's up?" The sergeant looked at him standing pondering.

"The girl that's staying here, the one being protected at all costs, wasn't her father with them the night they were allegedly raped?"

"But they were hypnotized. Surely you don't think he's into that?"

Jones raised his eyebrows. "Well, somebody is. Find out where he was last night, when you leave here."

They both got down and started to examine the floor, looking for the tiniest scrap that could be sent to forensic. Williams was in front of the fireplace when he heard a muffled exclamation. Looking up he saw Jones's head pop over the back of the settee.

"Come here".

Williams scrambled up and hurried to where the older man was on his knees.

"What is it?"

Jones nodded in the direction of the floor. "Smell. Down there."

Williams sniffed at the carpet. "I can't smell anything."

"Try again."

This time the slightest aroma floated up his nostrils. "What is it?"

Jones shook his head. "Don't know, but I've smelt it before. Trouble is, I can't remember where, or on whom."

Williams was sniffing all around. "It seems a bit stronger on the back of the settee, but then it's only very faint."

"Shame we can't bag that." Jones got up. "Better let the mother back in " and he got up and went to the kitchen to let Beth bring in the tea.

Both men smiled as she put the tray on a small table. After the usual exchange of how they liked it, the sergeant said "While it's cooling, may I show the Chief upstairs?"

She hesitated for a moment then nodded. "Yes, should I come as well, perhaps I could-----"

"No, no we'll be fine Mrs. Stokes." The Chief was already on his way and held up his hand in a gesture to make her stay where she was.

Left alone, Beth felt moved to tears. It all seemed so sordid and she wished with all her heart that none of it had ever happened. "Robert" she thought, "I must tell Robert." She picked up the phone and dialled his work number to leave a message for him to ring her, but she was put through to him straight away. Quickly she explained what had happened and he immediately scolded her for not having informed him the night before.

She pointed out that if he had come dashing round, which they both knew he would, Margaret would have guessed something more sinister was afoot. Reluctantly he agreed she was right, but assured her he would be there at lunch time.

"Won't Madge mind?" She almost smiled at the thought.

"Nothing to do with her. See you soon".

As she replaced the receiver, the two officers came back into the room.

"Well?" she enquired.

"Nothing that we can see." The Chief had had a good nose around in the girls' rooms, for any clue to them having any male associations, but had drawn a blank.

"Oh by the way," Beth said "I've told Margaret's father, I thought it only right."

"Oh." The Chief tried not to show his disappointment. He had wanted to spring it on Bradley without prior warning and judge his reaction, but the silly woman had ruined that. Instead he said "Yes, quite right. What did he say?"

"He's coming round to see me at lunch time and I can tell him more then."

The two men shot glances at each other. "Would you mind if we popped back then?" the sergeant tried to make it sound casual but Beth picked up something in his tone.

"Why? You don't think he had anything to do with this? I remember what you put him through before."

"Mrs. Stokes, You are Lizzie's mother, it seems only right that we should speak to one of Margaret's parents, and her father would be fine. Or perhaps we should just talk straight to the girl herself." He got the reaction he expected.

"No. No. You can't, she's doing so well, you don't realize the mental torment she's been through." She was really agitated and the sergeant stepped in to calm her.

"We understand. Look, let's all have a talk to Mr. Bradley, and then we'll take it from there. Alright?"

She nodded feeling she had betrayed Robert and she prayed he wouldn't think she had arranged this. So she made up her mind that, as soon as these two had gone, she would ring him again and warn him. It was the least she could do.

CHAPTER 13

Johhahn's hatred of his leader was growing, but the knowledge that he would soon overthrow him and gain almighty power spurred him on like a being possessed.

Jenny was aware of this activity. She had done many double switches, undetected, and been able to view the hybrids many times. When Johhahn tended his special crop, she had observed the difference in these six and was determined to release the creatures at her earliest opportunity. Also, with them destroyed, Johhahn would have no hold over his master and could easily be banished to spend the rest of his existence in torment and misery. In earthly terms, in hell.

It had not gone unnoticed on Eden, that Zargot was spending more time on earth, stirring up the wanton lust in the covens, making the pathetic life forms crave more and more enjoyment. It was like a drug, and they were all now well and truly hooked.

But this concentration of his attention could be his downfall, for, although he could thought travel in an instant, while he was enjoying the pleasures of those supplying his needs, he was in no hurry to abandon such delights.

Jenny was always ready to be one step ahead, but her plan did not meet with her father's instant approval.

"If you lay a bait for him, be it you or one of our ultimates, you are no better than he, you sink to his level."

"But Father. If I can be sure he cannot return to Zargon, or the holding area, it gives me the time to destroy the hybrids, or at least some of them in particular. The Schynings are only too glad to help me."

Her Father paused in thought. "I do not need to ask who you are thinking of dispatching." He imagined it would be Marie.

Jenny hesitated. "It's Graham Father."

"Graham!"

"He would take on female form for a short time. He has completed his seven proper lives on earth so this would be merely a temporary visitation, which we only use in extreme circumstances."

Her father's thought tone was severe. "I am aware of the technicalities."

There was a pause.

"Well, Father?"

"If you are asking for my blessing child," the pause seemed endless but she waited patiently. "I think you are fighting evil with more evil, not good, but I am sure of the sincerity of your intentions, so my love and protection goes with you and those assisting you."

This was as much as she could hope for, and wasted no time contacting her soul mate.

"I want to pull Marie and Matthew in on this," she imparted. "Firstly Matthew can be the main contact with the Schynings, and I want Marie to oversee any unusual happenings and report back."

"Good idea." Graham was pleased to be working so closely with Jenny again. "When do we move?"

"This coming earth night. Are you ready for such a task?"

Graham sent out positive thought waves. "Certainly. But who is the target?"

"Zena."

"What?" Graham quite expected it to be Vedron or one similar.

For every Vedron or Zena, there were thousands like them now operating their sordid little practices in every county in the British Isles, in Europe, Australia, America, the various islands dotted around the globe, and then out on to the far reaching planets. This was no longer a pleasant little game, a newly found past-time but a widespread evil reproducing itself as it travelled. And Zargot was at the helm.

Jenny was a little amused at Graham's reaction. "Thought you might find it a bit of a shock.."

"But why not go for Vedron, if I'm taking on female form?"

"Because Vedron's attentions are directed to one being, Lizzie. It may take longer to veer him away, if he ever does. Zena on the other hand is not quite so fussy. If it's offered, she will take it."

"But I thought she had this Bradley woman."

"Hmm. But having observed the last ritual, with some distaste I may say, I feel she is tiring of the creature. A nice fresh change may be just what she is seeking."

"Me." Graham's thought was a little weak.

Jenny affirmed.

"Tonight." Graham was hoping he could perform as a woman, not knowing just what was before him.

Jenny was serious now. "The main objective is to draw Zargot without him suspecting. We know he takes over the Vexons at the crucial moment of pleasure, that should give you enough cover. His lust should cloak any recognition."

"And I will be alone?"

"Yes, it's essential. I will be waiting for Marie's indication that Zargot is where we want him, then Matthew will call in the Schynings to the holding zone."

"But" she continued, "you must 'mind clear', concentrate only on the business in hand."

And so the plan was ready.

Madge Bradley lay sprawled across the double bed now only used by her. She felt ill, but couldn't explain in what way. This new little game, which at first had brought some colour into her humdrum life, was taking over, ruling her. Although if she was honest, it was Zena who had got the hold on her. Madge couldn't quite determine whether it was extreme pleasure, extreme fear or mere possession that now held her in its grip. She wasn't sure if she wanted to continue, but knew that the choice was no longer hers.

As she lay there aching from every limb, the scratches on her thighs smarting, she wondered what would happen if she said she didn't want to partake any more. She pushed the thought from her brain immediately, self preservation kicking into gear. You didn't tell Zena, you obeyed, if you valued your weak miserable little life.

Slowly, she pulled herself up and almost crawled to the bathroom. As she caught sight of her drained face in the mirror she shuddered. The normally clean, fairly well groomed woman had been replaced with a haggard well used slut, whose eyes appeared sunk into her cheeks, and traces of old make up emerging from the lines around her neck.

"A bath" she decided, "I'll have a long soak. Then I'll feel better." As the warm suds rose she slipped out of her remaining clothes and eased herself gently into the tub. As the essences reached between her legs she winced at the pain, grimacing at the memory of the various things that had been pushed up into her. Gradually she lay back and let the smooth relaxing waters float over her.

Suddenly she felt a pressure on her head, and her face was being pushed below the waterline. Her chin, followed by her nostrils and then her eyes until her whole face was submerged. Frantically she struggled grasping up at the edge of the bath to pull herself free, and fighting to hold her breath. As the pressure was realized she came up choking, gasping and lay with her head hanging over the side until she felt she could breathe normally. But the relief was overshadowed by the image she had received as she felt the hold go. It was the same green mist that she was only too familiar with, and in the mist she saw Zena's face merging with another horrible face.

She knew that this was just a warning. They could have killed her there and then, and nobody would have known the reason. Terror swept through her body as she wished with all her heart she had never started this practice. But it was too late for regrets.

Beth would have been none too pleased to learn that Det.Ch.Insp. Jones and his companion had gone straight round to Lizzie's place of work. Matron was quite co-operative but stressed that Lizzie had work to do and could they please be as quick as possible.

The men spent ten minutes talking to the girl, but gleaned little. She confirmed that neither she nor Margaret could remember anything after her mother left, until the time when they both woke up together.

Vernon Treloar was working in the garden, but keeping a keen eye on the visit. Lizzie waved in friendly fashion to him.

"Who's that?" The chief asked.

"Oh that's Vernon," Lizzie waved again, "he does odd jobs and stuff about the place."

Det. Sgt. Williams leaned forward and said in a mischievous manner "Not been out with him then?"
Lizzie threw back her head and laughed. "Him? Oh no he's too old. But he's very friendly and the old folks like him."

Knowing they would get no more out of her, the two men took their leave and left her to get on with her chores.

As they got into the car, Jones asked, "What was all that about?"
Williams turned to him. "What was what about?"
"You know all that 'been out with him' bit?"
Williams sighed. "Not sure. But did you notice how he was studying us?"
"Not particularly."
"I just got the feeling he wasn't too happy about us being there. Wanted to know what was going on."
The chief shrugged. "Well I don't think he's the boy friend, if she's got one."
"Oh no nothing like that. But here's a thought. Working there, couldn't he just have access to chloroform?"

Jones had started the car but switched off the engine. "Come on. Where's your thought going?"
"Well, it maybe nothing, but he works with the girl, knows her movements. She's very forthcoming and open. And, although it may be nothing, one of the old dears died recently. You remember one of the strange cases."
Jones looked at him. "And you think there could be some connection?"
"Oh I don't know. It was just something in the way he was staring at us."
Jones grunted. "Hm. Let's not dismiss it. We're seeing the Bradley chap soon. Let's mull it all over after that."

The men travelled in silence, both weighing up this new lead in their own way.

Zargot was busy on a small space area just off Neptune inhabited by a small insignificant race of what he called space rubbish. The beings were no more than two feet high, bore little resemblance to humans and sported little intelligence. The evil one was aware of their lack of evolution, but was prepared to plant his malignant seeds early in their development, thus spawning a new race of Zargs to replace any natural wastage of trouble makers. If this almighty entity felt his grip slipping in any area, he was quick to replace it from his many back up areas, many having been nurtured over centuries until the right time demanded their release.

Knowing his master was occupied, Johhahn decided to take the opportunity to visit his J children. He had recently been receiving signals from them, pulling him towards them, but he had to space out his visits so as not to arouse his leaders suspicions any more than necessary.

Stirring up a moment of turmoil amongst his fellow ultimates, he waited for them all to be engrossed in savage combat, then unnoticed, transported to the holding zone.

He immediately went to the J six positions and was astounded to find them all empty. His first reaction was that Zargot had been there before him and dispatched the six without his knowledge. Anger filled his being. Was that what his children were trying to tell him? Were they trying to warn him?

As if in answer, he felt himself swung round and moved down the rows at speed, until just as quickly he was halted. Relief spread over his ideal as he came face to face with J1, but just as quickly felt panic as he realized these creatures were becoming self motivated. They were no longer obeying his commands as he had so carefully planned, but were now trying to command him, and succeeding.

With all his evil power he wrenched his will away from them, attempting to take control. He slowly looked into the eye slits of each of them, and as he did, the apertures widened until he felt he would be swallowed into the unseen depths. He knew at this moment, that if he did not act immediately against Zargot, his chance would be gone, and these festering souls would take him over.

He could only guess that the J hybrids had moved themselves into a position vacated by six other guinea pigs, and while that didn't seem too important, it did make him wonder as to the full extent of their uncontrolled ability, and at what speed they were developing.

Quickly he manoeuvered them to the launch position and placed two hybrids in each capsule. He felt the animosity emitting from them as a combined show of hatred. Johhahn took his position at the control console, and using two of the zombie hybrids to press the buttons, plotted a flight path straight towards Zargot's current position. As the crafts left, carrying the six monsters of his creation, he indulged in the relief that they would never return.

His experiment had failed this time, but having achieved so much, he would try again, until all evil powers would be under his control.

Beth had a pot of tea made when Robert tapped on her door. She had managed to warn him of the police officers' visit, but he had shrugged it off knowing he had nothing whatever to hide. If fact he welcomed the chance for them to learn some true facts and thus get them off his back.

"Oh Robert, I'm so pleased you could come." She felt strong as this man took her in his arms and hugged her for longer than she expected.

"I'd have been here before, you know that. Oh Beth how are the girls?"

"Alright." she smiled up at him. "Lizzie's fine considering, and Margaret seems quite oblivious of it all."

"That's thanks to you two." Robert hugged her again.

They sat down and Beth produced some sandwiches with the tea. "Thought you'd need a snack."

Robert put his hand on her knee and looked at her lovingly. Much against her will, she drew away.

"What does Madge say?" she asked quickly.

"Beth, let's not talk about Madge, not now."

"But" Beth attempted a girlish laugh "she's your wife, Margaret's mother, we can't forget she exists. I'm surprised she hasn't rung really. Even if it was to blame me."

"Beth." Robert stopped her flow. "There is much going on. I can't say too much at the moment, but I don't think Madge is interested in Margaret, or me or you."

"What are you saying?"

"Leave it for now; let's deal with the matter in hand. I'll tell you when I know more about what is going on."

Beth thought for a moment. "Well, I'm certainly intrigued."

Robert was saved from elaborating further, by the arrival of Messrs. Jones and Williams. They accepted the offered tea, but asked Beth to remain when she asked if they would like to see Robert alone.

"You are aware of why we are here Mr. Bradley?" The Chief wasted no time in getting down to brass tacks.

"Yes, Beth, um, Mrs. Stokes told me briefly." He looked from one to the other.

Jones eyed him. "Just as a matter of routine you understand sir, but could you just confirm your whereabouts last night."

"Certainly, I was at home all evening."

"With whom?" Sgt Williams slipped the question in almost unnoticed.

Robert turned to him, "No-one."

"So you can't prove it?" Jones seemed as though he had expected this. "Where was your wife sir?"

"Out. Oh for goodness sake. Look I was watching a documentary, anyway" as sudden recognition leaped into his mind he said "I rang here."

Everyone in the room looked at him.

"When?" Beth was first to ask. "You didn't say before."

The chief, not wanting to be cut out of his questioning said "Go on Mr. Bradley. What time was that?"

Robert looked at them all. "I'd just finished watching the programme, Madge was out, as usual, and I thought I'd give Beth a ring. We often talk you know, about Margaret and such."

"That's right officer, he's a very caring father." Beth nodded at the men, but then said, "But I was out Robert."

"Yes I know that now, but I didn't then. Anyway, there was no reply, which I found a bit strange."

Williams cut in, "So we can work out the time, when your programme finished, and we can check the call through the telephone people."

Robert looked a little relieved. "You certainly can." But his face fell a little when Jones intervened, "Of course that will confirm that a call was made from your number, but not by whom."

A slight hush fell upon the room, but then Jones said "It could be very useful." They all waited for him to continue. "It pins it down doesn't it?" Robert shook his head, "Pins what down exactly?"

Again the chief paused, mainly to assure he had everyone's attention.
"So Mrs. Stokes you left at --?"
"Oo, just after seven, I don't know to the minute."
"That's near enough." Jones nodded, then turned to Robert. "And the programme you were watching finished at----?"
"It would have been half past eight come the think of it. It was a nature thing. Then I got a drink, say five minutes or so then rang Beth."

Williams had been jotting down the facts with Jones looking over his shoulder. The sergeant, still looking at the paper summed up, "So, Mrs. Stokes goes out about seven o'clock, Mr. Bradley rings approx. 8.35, but nobody knows about it?"
"Just a minute, are you saying----?" Robert sat forward but the sergeant held up his hand.
"If the girls were put under again, it narrows it down to this hour and a half."

Beth's mouth opened but closed again. The horror of somebody being in her house, taking over the girls will was becoming so repulsive; she hoped she had the strength to cope with it.

The chief noticed her distress and said "We'll get him Mrs. Stokes, we know it's painful, and you are being very helpful."
"I'm sorry, it's just the thought ---"
The older man nodded understandingly. He had daughters of his own and could identify with her feelings. It crossed his mind that Bradley was also a father, but to his mind the man had not yet been completed cleared of suspicion.

"So nobody answered the phone Mr. Bradley?" The chief looked questioningly at him.
"No, I've told you, there was nobody here---" his voice trailed off "but there was, this is what you are saying." The officers let the recognition sink in and let him continue. "Oh God Beth, if only I'd come round, I could have caught him." He was nearly sobbing and Beth tried to comfort him.
"Robert, don't blame yourself."
"But if I could have got my hands on that fiend that put Margaret through this, and your Lizzie---"he dropped his face into his hands his body shaking.

At a signal from Jones, the officers got to their feet. "I think that's enough for now. Thank you both very much. We'll let you know when we get the results of the tests."

Beth composed herself enough to show the officers out, then ran back to where Robert had still not moved. Together they hugged each other and cried many pent up tears, unashamed in their mutual sadness and unspoken love.

As the policemen left, Williams said "Just what was the question you wanted to ask?"

Jones gave him a knowing look as they got into the car. "Smart ass."

Williams smiled and retorted "You haven't answered my question."

"I just wanted to know," he paused and smiled.

"Go on."

"I just wanted to know if you can hypnotize somebody as effectively down the phone as you can face to face."

"I'm glad you didn't ask him that?" Williams was a little astounded at the chief's train of thought.

"Well, we'll see what the results bring. Be interesting to see if the seminal stains match the last attack. And I think they will."

Williams said positively, "And they were not the same as Bradley's remember, because he was tested."

"Oh I remember," the chief smiled to himself. "I also remember something else." He snapped his fingers.

"What?"

"The smell. It isn't one particular pong. It's a mixture of men's toiletries, and a slight whiff of something else. It's been on all the ones interviewed in one area, Minster Lovell, and I bet if you check with the police surgeon, it was on Bradley when he examined him."

"You still don't trust him do you? Well I believe he is innocent. I think he is a distressed father who would stop at nothing to get his hands on his daughter's attacker. That's what I think."

The chief drove off smiling. "Oh I didn't say I didn't trust him?"

CHAPTER 14

The message reached Jenny in an instant. There was activity at the holding zone near Zargon. "Oh no. Not yet." was her first reaction. This coming earth night she was set to trap Zargot on earth while she attended to things, namely the poor wretches trapped in the Z-tombs, the zombies. Tonight she would free them for ever and nothing would stop her.

She was in conference on Eden with her closest ultimates. "How many?" It was unbelievable that only three craft had been dispatched which meant that either three or six hybrids were used.

The reply came from Marie. "Yes only three, and they were sent to Neptunii."

"But why? It doesn't make sense. Unless..." She did a double switch to the holding zone and almost instantly reported "So that's it."

"What?" rippled through the spirals.

"It's not himself. It's that underling of his. This could have been almost what we wanted, a distraction, but the trouble is it's too close to home."

"What is the answer?" Matthew thought.

"We don't want him hovering over the rest. Just a minute. Got to re-check something. Again she double switched.

"Strange."

"What is?" All the ultimates wondered.

"On the first switch, I was sure the special six had gone. But on the second switch, they appear to be back."

"Probably done their job. Maybe a test run." Marie offered.

"I'm not happy with it," Jenny sent the ripple through the levels requesting all ideals to report the slightest wave of unrest.

"We will operate this coming earth night as planned" she ordered, "but with extreme caution."

Zena was in need of excitement. Her recent triumphant results with the other world had fired her enthusiasm, her feeling of supreme power. Except for one thing. Whilst she revelled in the terror on the faces of Mandy and Deana when the entities engulfed the meetings, she was aware of a certain reluctance stemming from Madge. The woman had seemed willing enough at first, they always did, these boring little people in search of thrills and excitement, until the practices became too scary for their capabilities. Then they wanted out.

The high priestess had often been forced to use all her own wiles together with a helpful nudge from the other side, to keep lips sealed, and thus protect her secrets from a prying outside world. Experience had taught her to spot the signs, and she was therefore ready to ditch her latest conquest, but only when she had found a suitable replacement. And Jenny was only too willing to provide the perfect specimen.

So Zena lost no time in contacting her two sentinels, warning them that unless they found her suitable prey immediately, their own pleasures would be terminated. Little did they know how easy it would be.

Zena also rang Madge and told her to be ready for another session that night.

"But I can't Zena," Madge was at the lowest possible ebb. "I'm ill, I couldn't stand it, not tonight."

The voice at the other end of the telephone snapped out its demand.

"You know by now my girl, that you do as you are bid, or else-----"

"Yes,--yes-- I'm sorry, I mean, I'll be there." She sobbed.

"Well, of course you will." The conversation was ended.

The smile on the priestess' face was more of a sadistic smirk as she replaced the receiver. "What a disappointment she was." She revelled in the past tense, eagerly looking forward to her next target, whoever it would be.

Beth was angry. "They did what?" Lizzie was happily telling her mother about the police visit to the nursing home and couldn't quite understand the reaction.

"But Mum they were very nice. And they haven't bothered Margaret, and that's the most important thing isn't it?"

Beth hugged her. "What a sweet nature you have, Lizzie, so like your Dad."

Making the most of Margaret's absence, Beth quickly told Lizzie about the officer's visits to her and the clothes going for forensic examination.

"We don't have to tell Margaret do we?" Lizzie implored.

"Well not at present any way." Suddenly a thought struck her. "Oh God, I hope they didn't go to see her at work, like they did you." Then after a second thought, "I wouldn't put it past them."

She looked at Lizzie tenderly. "You know, I think they still believed Margaret's dad had something to do with it."

"But he didn't." The girl was emphatic. Beth looked at her and sat her down.

Gently she said "How are you so sure Lizzie?"

"I don't know, but I just know it wasn't him. But I feel as though I know the person. That's sounds silly doesn't it, I mean, I don't know who it was and yet-----"

"Yes dear. Try and think."

After deep thought she shook her head. "Sorry Mum, it's sort of there, but it won't come."

"It's alright dear. But there is just one thing."

"Yes."

"Last night, sometime when you were obviously under, you know, probably hypnotized again, do you remember the phone going?"

Lizzie jumped. "The phone."

Beth was excited "Yes."

"It - it seemed to be when we woke up. I forgot all about it, but now you say, it must have been the ringing that woke me. Don't you think so Mum?"

"So he'd gone then." Beth mulled it over in her mind. If everything had already happened by 8.35pm, the attacker had wasted no time after she had gone out before making his move.

A chill ran through her veins. He was probably watching, and waiting. Could it be someone they knew? Could Lizzie unwittingly be inviting someone she trusted into their home?

They were interrupted by Margaret's arrival. "Sorry I'm late, I've just been talking to a person." Beth was about to pass it over with relief that the girl was alright, but caution suddenly raised its head in view of recent events.

Lightly she asked, "Oh, who was that dear?" Margaret giggled and sat by Lizzie. "Oh you should have seen her, long blond hair and short shirt and all made up. She was a mess."

The two thought this a huge joke, but Beth asked "What did she want?"

Margaret shrugged. "Funny really, asked if I knew the way to the nature park, then asked if I would go and show her where it was."

For some reason Beth was disturbed. Could this have anything to do with the rape? "You didn't go dear?"

"Good gracious no." Margaret laughed again. "I wouldn't be seen with a tart like that. Said her name was Mandy." The two hooted again. Beth felt relief at the girls' reaction, as she obviously had not been disturbed by it. But the woman made a mental note to mention it to the sergeant as soon as she could.

Vedron felt safe. He had pulled off a dangerous operation successfully. To have ventured into the home of the object of his desire, and leave undetected, unrecognized gave him a thrill. But this fuelled his lust to have Lizzie alone, unhypnotized and giving herself willingly to him.

A slight apprehension hit him as he recalled the visit of the two police to the nursing home. He must find out why they were talking to Lizzie. Obviously from her reactions she seemed to be in no distress, and she shouldn't have remembered anything about the sexual side as his hypnotic powers had never failed before. He hadn't even needed to use the chloroform, a useful standby, but both females had reacted perfectly.

This should have made the Vexon determined to exercise full caution in the future, but the sexual drive of lust and possession always came to the fore with this species, often causing their downfall.

Zargot was quite content to let Vedron dive headlong into the next encounter, happily taking over at the right moment and savouring the ecstasy through the host's body. He was slowly entering Lizzie's ideal, planting the evil seeds of desire, making her crave for something, but not knowing what.

His attention was momentarily turned to Zena. Drawn by her sadistic revenge over the disappointment of the Madge creature, she was equally excited over the prospect of her next 'meal' as she called it.

Zargot decided to return that night and witness the happening. The portal was wide enough to attract all the entities she wished to muster, but he would add a few of his own. Zena, the high priestess who loved to play with her mice, would in turn be the plaything of the almighty cat, Zargot.

Jenny summoned her immediate workers. "It's time to make a move Graham."

"But it's still earth day." Graham was in no hurry to take on the form of the seductress.

"And her servants are searching for fresh pasture." She was aware of Mandy's attempt on securing Margaret, although for the blonds' sake it was lucky to have failed as Zena would have been not too pleased at being offered Madge's offspring. The girls could be quite useless at times.

"Time for us to make it easy for them Graham." Jenny indicated towards earth. "Go and make the necessary arrangements for later, then return here."

With a quick farewell he was gone, and Jenny immediately called Marie and Matthew to conference to finalize the plans for the hours ahead.

Graham quickly located Mandy who was still roaming Burford in the hopes of finding a suitable replacement for her leader.

It was fairly quiet at this time of year, not many tourists during the autumn. The surrounding villages offered little in the way of fresh pickings, and most of the residents knew each other, so she would stand out considerably. She could have travelled over to Bourton, but she preferred her own territory, and had often been warned off someone else's patch.

It was just after lunch. She had just had a sandwich and a drink in one of the local pubs and was sitting in her car near the old grammar school deciding on her next move. Today had not gone very well, but she dare not return empty handed.

In her rear view mirror she caught sight of a woman approaching over the small bridge which spanned the river.
"Oh my God, if this isn't heaven sent." she gasped, but just as quickly thought "this has got to be too good to be true."

As the woman approached she slowly wound down the window to get a good view of her. She was in her late thirties, quite well dressed with shoulder length fair hair. As she drew level with the car, she stopped and fiddled with a strap on her sandal.

Mandy leaned out. "Got a problem love?" The other woman started as though she hadn't noticed she was being observed.
"Oh, it's these shoes, they're killing me, silly to wear them really."
Mandy couldn't believe her luck. "Hey, want to take the weight off a minute?"
"Oh, could I? I mean that's awfully decent of you."

As the woman tottered round to the passenger seat Mandy thought "Oh one of the jolly hockey sticks brigade. Should suit her majesty down to the ground."

"Oh, this is so kind of you." The visitor smiled sweetly at Mandy who said "That's O.K. done it myself many times. I'm Mandy by the way."
"Hello. I'm Hannah. Would you mind terribly if I took my shoes off for a minute?"

The thought crossed Mandy's mind that this creature could be taking off a lot more than her skimpy shoes if all went well. Calmly she said "Be my guest." Then after a moment "You weren't out walking in those?"
Hannah looked a little sheepish. "Sounds silly I know, but I didn't intend to go far, but I always like to look at the river. I suppose it's more the weather for boots really." She rubbed her feet before adding, "I do hope I can get them back on now."

Mandy jumped at this opportunity never suspecting it was being cleverly stage managed. "Hey, why don't I give you a lift?"
"Oh I couldn't impose, you've been so kind already and---"
"Think nothing of it old girl" was the reply as she started the engine, "Where do you live?"

This one had to be played carefully. "Oh I'm staying at the hotel on Sheep Street, but I don't want to impose really."

Mandy had already pulled into the main stream of traffic and was heading up the hill. "Know anybody much around here?"

Hannah went a little coy. "No, I'm only visiting a relative, and there doesn't seem much to do in the evenings, so I'm at a bit of a loose end."

Mandy was too busy patting herself on the proverbial back to realize she was walking straight into the trap. Before bidding farewell, she had arranged to collect Hannah that evening for a bit of old schoolgirl jollity, as she put it. She waved her new friend goodbye, but would have been astounded to learn that, instead of entering the hotel, the woman had taken the side path, and then vanished.

CHAPTER 15

Johhahn's ideal shuddered mentally as he viewed his J hybrids all dangling apparently lifelessly in their original spaces. When he had dispatched them on their last flight, he had programmed their self destruction, so what had gone wrong? The answer hit him as though it had come from the beings themselves. They had over-ridden the commands and taken control of the crafts of their own accord, and returned to base to continue their own project.

He quaked at the thought, not knowing to what lengths these things would go, if in fact there was a limit to their ever growing evil intentions.

One thing was certain; their main target appeared to be him, their creator. Well, he must take positive action now, there was no time to lose.

Quickly he confirmed Zargot's location. The leader was engrossed on Neptunii nurturing his 'rubbish'. The almighty one had been very perturbed at the visitation of the three craft recently, and suspected Johhahn of trying to destroy his nursery. If things had gone according to plan, the crafts would have burned out long before reaching the destination and therefore not aroused Zargot's suspicions further. But the clever hybrids had de-programmed the destruct mechanism and purposely flown on a path which Zargot could not possibly miss.

Being aware of the flights, Zargot had thought transferred to the leading ship and commanded the J1 hybrid to alter course and return to the holding zone. This order was passed to the other two. Johhahn, being so stunned by the return, never guessed that his evil ruler was behind the move.

Satisfied that he would not be interrupted until his task was completed, the lower ultimate stared deep into the eye slits of the six. "This time," he revelled in the control he thought he now had "this time, you will not return. Your miserable existence is about to end, you fools.

With me, we could have ruled everything, space, time, eternity, but you destroyed that."

Suddenly Johhahn was aware that the hybrids no longer hung lifeless in position. They were all round him, closing in, squeezing his ideal to a thread. Utter terror engulfed him and he screamed for the power of Zargot to free him from the stifling pressure which now threatened his ultimate existence.

With relief he felt a power above drawing him upwards, stretching his being like a rubber band until he was sucked out at tremendous speed. But his relief was short lived.

The voice of the evil one echoed through the surrounding space. "Did you really think you could overthrow the powerful one, you meager scrap of nothingness?"

Johhahn knew it would be no good pleading for he knew his fate. In an instant, Zargot had banished the being to a black hole area on the outer limits of the galaxy. An area from which nothing could escape, even light. Here the outcast would be crushed into the mass, never to be free again. Such was the wrath of Zargot.

The stage was being set for the forthcoming night. Matthew was already in contact with the Schynings who were hovering nearby awaiting the call. Marie, in her usual efficient manner, had lesser ideals stationed at strategic points to report immediately of anything unusual, or warn of danger. Jenny was staying on Eden until the very last moment, and therefore not giving Zargot any indication of the operation.

The news of Johhahn's dismissal had hit Eden like a shock wave, and Jenny hoped this would not detract the evil one from pursuing his earthly pleasures.

On earth, the players were making their own plans for the evening. Robert was going round to Beth's. The girls were quite happy to stay in which brought relief to both parents and they all decided to settle down and watch a film.

Madge was going out as usual, but this time against her will. At least with her husband out of the way she would not have any of the normal explaining to do. Reluctantly, she put on her make up and tight clothes, and swallowed some pills. She didn't really know why, but she hoped it might help to blot out anything unpleasant.

Mandy had rung Zena to brag of her conquest, and then phoned Deana to go through it all again.

"Just as well you found something, I've had no joy." Deana sounded uninterested at first, wishing she had been the one to capture the bait, but secretly was relieved as it let her off the hook for the time being. Next time, there was always next time.

Zena was excited at the prospect of pastures new. But first she had to dispense with the other little problem, although from experience it should prove to be quite an enjoyable little past-time.

Vedron was frustrated. He needed to move in on Lizzie to satisfy his growing desires. He had no plans set, but stood alone scheming as to how he could achieve his goal.

Unaware of the impending supernatural events, Det.Ch.Insp. Jones had arranged to visit Det.Sgt.Williams that evening to try and piece together the local happenings and fit them into the ever growing jig-saw of evil practices.

Following Beth's 'phone call to the sergeant concerning Margaret's encounter with Mandy, Williams had dug out the report he had taken from his friend Barry Timms. He felt that things were falling into line, and above all, he knew that soon Robert Bradley's name would be cleared. But he was still uneasy over the odd job man at the nursing home, Treloar wasn't it? The officer didn't know the connection, but instinct told him there was one, and he would dig it out somehow.

Graham, as Hannah, was due to be picked up by Mandy at 7.30pm. 'She' had been told there would be five in the car, so they would have to squeeze up a bit, but not to worry as one may not be returning with them. "Going by other means" was how it was put. To any mere mortal the explanation would have been acceptable, but in the circumstances Hannah saw beyond the obvious and caution was to the fore.

Graham had told Jenny that he did not want to arrive at the destination until the last minute which was agreed.

There was one more player to arrive, also not from earthly source, but he would make a grand entrance, in more ways than one, Zargot.

With the dispatch of Johhahn, there had been a scramble among the lesser entities to fill the empty space. This would have been unheard of on Eden as the ultimates were not bent on destruction and super power, but on Zargon things were very different. The evil leader had the final say on any movement, but not before great deliberation. If he promoted a being with no fight, no mental stamina, it would be down trodden in no time by the existing forces. On the other hand, if he opted for one more of his own thinking, he could have another Johhahn to contend with

He surveyed the cosmos. Better to choose one who had been out of any physical form for some time, as they would be acclimatized ready for their new role. His attention was drawn to a Zarg known as Klee. As on Eden, the ideals were of neither sex but had taken both forms when in body, however Klee was predominantly female, appeared young in existence, but could call on more experience than any of the lower spiral.

She had been instrumental in causing much destruction around the galaxy, all of which had been carefully noted by her master, much to the dislike of the ultimates on both spirals.

Zargot had decided. Klee would do very nicely. Probably knock the others into shape, and if not it would certainly provide him with much entertainment. However, he would let them all churn it over for a while. First he would enjoy the earth happenings tonight, which promised to be very fulfilling.

"I'll go." Beth was on her feet as she heard Robert's knock on the door. She still had a slight hang up over Lizzie opening the door to a stranger. "Silly" she told herself," it's all in your mind."

"Hello you three beautiful girls." Robert's smile brought instant relief to Beth who pretended to blush a little. Margaret was sitting on the settee with Lizzie as usual, and both heads turned and beamed at the parents.

"He means you really Mum" Lizzie called and nudged her friend.

"Oh yes, that's right isn't it Dad?" Margaret only just uttered the words then collapsed with Lizzie in a heap.

Beth looked at them, and then to the man standing very close to her. "What do you make of them?"

"Oh they're just being naughty, as usual," he laughed as he hurried over to the back of the settee and playfully tousled their hair. This caused more screams of mirth, and Beth felt so happy at the relaxed atmosphere, wishing, hoping-- but no she must put such thoughts from her mind for now. They certainly made a very happy family, but there was one flaw, Madge.

Robert made himself comfortable in one of the armchairs having similar thoughts. When he was sure of what Madge was up to, he would confide in Beth, but for now nothing at all was going to spoil this wonderful evening.

"Mum's made a lovely pie for us for later." Lizzie looked like a little girl about to have a rare treat and Robert warmed to the simple out-look on life of this offspring of the woman he had always loved. His attention was turned to his own daughter who added "Yes, Auntie Beth says I can have a big piece."

Beth switched on the television and joined the girls. "Oh this is so nice," she breathed not daring to look at Robert in case she gave more away than she should.

So this happy little group settled in for a pleasant evening, completely unaware of the turmoil about to take place around them.

Zargot had many uses for the hybrids, varying orders depending on their destination at the time. He was planning to send batches of six crafts each containing two hybrids to the Saturn area to destroy newly formed colonies. The craft were now fitted with deadly rays which could wipe out a space or earth city in an instant, cause widespread fires, or interfering with electrical sources or telecommunications, and especially satellite links.

The hybrids were programmed to press controls, either in advance, almost like being on auto pilot, or by remote control signals from Zargon itself. Therefore, any surprise tactic could be dealt with.

It occurred to him that it would be fun to use one or two around the many earth rituals taking place that night. It was almost like a menu spread before him. Which to choose? He decided to be greedy and visit as many as possible, thus savouring the delights offered.

He had made it his business to learn of Lizzie's plans, much to his disappointment. Following his possession of Vedron, his appetite was whetted over this innocent submissive maid. It was his need of her that was driving Vedron to take her in unhypnotized form, so that she too could savour the pleasures that he, the almighty power, had to offer.

The idea played around his ideal, to send a hybrid down and let her think she had been abducted by an alien. Of course nobody would believe her story. He would use the Vexon's body to give him the physical pleasure he desperately desired whilst letting her have full vision of the hybrid. What a description her imaginative mind would produce.

However, that would have to wait for tonight. There were other delights in store, especially the lesbian Vexon who was going to extinguish one flame in favour of a fresh one. He'd concentrate on that location primarily. That should be excellent for a starter, and what an ideal place to introduce a hybrid. That should really add a bit of fun. The earthlings would probably think it had come through the portal. "Well, let them," he mused, "shouldn't meddle with what they don't understand."

Mandy collected Deana and Zena, and turned the car in the direction of where she would pick up Madge. They travelled in silence, knowing the high priestess did not take kindly to idle chatter but suddenly Mandy exclaimed, "She's not there!"

"What?" The anger rose in Zena's voice as she leaned between the two in the front of the car to peer into the gloom.

"Hang on." Deana pointed to a figure slowly approaching. "There she is."

"Tell her to hurry." Zena sat back in disgust.

Deana half got out of the car and beckoned. "Come on, what do you think you are playing at?"

Madge still did not hurry, but sauntered to the rear door and very deliberately got in alongside her mistress who eyed her up and down and retorted "That wasn't very clever." Then to Mandy, "Well, what are you hanging around for girl?"

The two in the front shot rapid glances at each other as they turned down the hill to collect Hannah. Zena looked ahead as she said curtly "You'll have to move up, we're introducing a newcomer tonight."

Madge sniffed. "I needn't have come then. I said I was ill." As soon as the words left her tongue she felt the woman turn towards her with all the hatred she had ever know directed at her.
"We have already discussed that." were the only words in reply.

"Is that her?" Deana looked surprised. "My, she's quite a stunner." Mandy halted the car at the side of the fifth member.

Graham had taken advice from Jenny and Marie as to his apparel, and they had settled on a figure hugging lilac wool suit with short skirt, and a flimsy scarf draped casually over the blond hair. As it was rather cold they opted for long white boots with chunkier heels than the silly sandals used earlier. But they had served the purpose in trapping the prey.

The effect met with instant approval from the Vexon whose mouth watered at the object now climbing in beside Madge. Mandy wasted no time in heading off in the direction of the ritual ground, secretly grateful that her successful catch had turned up.

As they turned off the main road to head into the country, they had to wait for a car coming the other way. If the other driver had only known the identity of the occupants and their intentions, he would have been elated, for it was none other than Det. Ch. Insp. Jones.

CHAPTER 16

Det.Sgt.Williams was poring over the reports at the police station, when his visiting superior entered the room.
"Oh, glad you're here sir," he started to rise from his chair, but Jones beckoned to him to remain seated.
"Let's keep this informal Roger," he said quickly pulling up another chair alongside. "Things seem to be moving, gathering momentum you might say."
"Oh?" Williams looked at him enquiringly. "Such as?"
"Well, I've been comparing findings, forensic results etc. and while a lot of the stuff is varied and doesn't piece together, you know the thing, one offs, dabblers," the sergeant nodded in agreement but wished the man would get to the point, "there seems to be a definite pattern especially round here."
"Can you be more specific?" The sergeant was eager to see if any of Jones' results tied in with his own deductions.

The chief opened his briefcase and spread papers across the desk. He was almost a little sheepish as he confessed "The seminal stains found on the Stokes girl's knickers were identical to those when she was raped first, and the same on her friend – um..“ he sorted through a couple of sheets until he grabbed the one he wanted "Margaret, Bradley's daughter."
"Well we guessed as much." Roger sensed what was coming next, and knew the chief was in no hurry to impart the knowledge, so he decided to do it for him. "And you are now going to tell me that the semen was not Robert Bradley's?"
Jones coughed uneasily. "Seems so. Well, no it wasn't his."
"So that let's him off the hook." The younger man tried to suppress a smile and quickly added, "Is there more because I've got something to show you?"

Taking advantage of changing the tone slightly, Jones continued "Yes, let me just go through these. According to various reports, the main activity causing concern around here is not from male attackers, but female."

Williams sat nodding, knowing this would only reinforce his own ideas.

"You don't seem that surprised," Jones hesitated.

"Not entirely, but go on."

"Several people have rung in but wanted to remain anonymous. They were where they shouldn't have been at night, but a few have centred on the same bit of road on the way to Carterton."

This wasn't quite what Roger had expected and he was intrigued. "Oh yes, where?"

"It's marked here look." He pointed to a small pencil circle on a map. "We don't know exactly, but it's on that stretch. A couple saw a car coming out of what looked like a field. The pair were parked with no lights in a gateway, so they wouldn't have been seen. I ask you?"

Williams smiled to himself, glad that the chief didn't ask what he thought they were doing! "Only the one couple reported it?" he asked.

"No. That's the point. At first I thought it must be a local farmer coming out of his land, but then another report came in, this time the chap gave his name but made us promise we wouldn't tell his wife."

"You're not telling me this was on the same night? Gateways must have been a bit full."

Jones eyed him for a moment then shrugged. "Yes. You know, there's more information out there from those who shouldn't be, if you know what I mean. Pity they don't all cough up, we'd have these evil bastards then."

Williams's brain was racing. "So, if we had a look in the daytime, perhaps we would find prints, tracks or something."

"That's what I was going to suggest. There have been four reports in all, the two on one night, like I said, and the others on different nights. All people having a crafty jump, cars well hidden, so the perpetrators wouldn't even know they'd been observed."

It was Williams' turn to take the stage, and in view of this recent development he knew he had the icing on the cake.

"I'll come back to the Bradley girl in a moment" he started, "but I think you'll find this interesting." He handed Jones the Barry Timms statement and sat back for the man to read the contents. Slowly Jones tapped the page, "You think this is one of them?"

With a slight nod, Roger leaned forward. "Mrs. Stokes told me that Margaret had been approached by a woman who said her name was Mandy, would you like a description?"

Jones shook his head in disbelief." Not the same as this?"

"The same."

"But hang on, you're going too fast young man. This statement of your friend Timms, I mean, she was after a man then, you're not trying to tell me she was enticing Margaret for the same purpose?"

"Who knows? Perhaps swings both ways. Anyway, there's more."

"Go on." Now it was Jones' turn to be hanging on every breath wondering what was unfolding.

"I was driving back over the bridge today, and saw a most attractive piece having trouble with some stupid shoes she was wearing."

"This is relevant I take it?" The chief thought the young officer was veering off the subject for a moment.

"It is, when I tell you that she got into a car. Would you like a description of the driver?"

Jones mouth opened but before he could reply, Williams pointed to the paper still in his hand, and continued. "I pulled round by the old grammar school and when I rejoined the High Street, I saw the two of them driving up the hill and turning into Sheep Street."

"Under our noses." Jones got a word in, "just round the corner from here."

"Either very brazen, or stupid, or, "Williams hesitated "innocent."

"Rubbish, too many coincidences. I want to know more about this Mandy person, and fast."

Williams let the dust settle for a moment then said pointedly to give full impact "There is something else I've uncovered."

Jones was getting up from his seat, but stopped half way and sat down again.

"You'd better let me have it."

"You know I wasn't altogether happy about the Treloar chap. Well, I've been digging."

"Don't tell me he's your Mandy, all we needs a transvestite in this mess."
"No. Not entirely."
"What?" Jones voice rose two octaves.
"It seems, that although he's lived around Burford all of his life, he has cropped up in other parts from time to time."
"In what way?" Jones stroked his chin.
"There was a case ten years ago near Bristol, where a man answering his description was accused of rape but got off. No substantial evidence. The girl was prone to hallucinations and it wasn't proved."
Jones shook his head "Why are you so sure it was him?"
"Because the man's name was Victor Taylor alias Vernon Treloar"
"But Bristol, what was he doing there" Jones looked stern "apart from attempted rape that is?"
"Nothing much. Was supposed to be on holiday. But that's not all."
"You have been busy. I bet the records department loves you."
Roger was in full swing. He could feel the net tightening round his prey.
"Closer to home, six years ago, A Vincent Traynor, alias Vernon Treloar was accused of rape in Leamington Spa. Always uses the same initials you see"
"Don't tell me, he got off again." The chief looked almost resigned to the lack of evidence which he was sure would be the result.
"Well, this was what I found intriguing. The girl gave a good description of the man, which fitted Treloar to the last detail, but failed to identify him as the attacker, so it never actually came to court"
Jones pulled a face. "I think I lost that somewhere."
Enjoying having his senior's full attention, Williams continued "The features, the clothing, everything described our man. But the girl, although she admitted he was familiar, said she couldn't be sure it was him. "
"Did she know him, or was it a chance thing?" Jones was pondering all the pieces of the jig saw, trying to sort them in his mind.
Roger smiled. "He was staying at the B & B run by the girl's mother. The attack is supposed to have taken place late at night. But this is the titbit that could have some bearing."
"Oh yes." Jones leaned forward.
"In her statement, the girl said that the man seemed familiar, she thought it was Mr.Traynor, but he looked different in some way. And, she

thought she fell asleep during the encounter, and when she woke up he had gone."

"Stains," Jones almost shouted, "what about the stains."

"There were none."

"What? Well that doesn't fit his present mode."

"There were none, because her pants were missing, never found. He must have removed the evidence."

"Hmm. Seemed a bit more careful then. Wonder why?"

The sergeant collected the papers together and tidied the desk.

"I'll get on to the Carterton road job tomorrow in the daylight, will you be coming down?"

"Only if you find something. But I'd keep it quiet for now, go alone."

"I was intending to. But tonight I want to observe our man, see if he leaves home, and if so where does he go. I'll also make some excuse to visit that nursing home again."

"Be careful," the chief warned, "if he's one of the players in this little game, he'll be cute. Don't give him grounds to suspect you're on to him."

"I will exercise the utmost caution" Roger assured him..

Both men got up to go their separate ways, but as his hand rested on the door handle Jones turned and said "Good work by the way."

As the car bearing the five women approached the destination, Zena scanned the darkness to make sure they were undetected as they turned down the track leading to the night's pleasure.

Graham had enlisted the aid of one of Marie's lesser known helpers to switch with him during the session, and thereby let himself remain undetected should Zargot appear and recognize his true ideal. But for now he remained in the appearance of Hannah, eagerly peering ahead.

As the car pulled to a halt, Zena broke the silence by addressing Madge in a somewhat vicious tone "Get out, you know what to do by now. So saying she opened the door and almost dragged the poor creature to the ground. Mandy turned and beckoned Hannah out of the opposite door. Graham thought he had better show some sign of interest and said "I can't see a thing, where are we going?"

"You'll find out," Deana chipped in, "you wanted some excitement didn't you dearie?"

They had all moved to the back of the car and were getting bags out of the boot. Mandy and Deana were soon attired in the usual fashion and Zena, already prepared merely slipped off her top coat to reveal her skin tight black outfit, which she completed with a long cloak.

"Oo this looks fun." Hannah giggled nervously.

"Don't you believe it" Madge tried to say but was stopped by the high priestess. "Ignore the girl, she's not well."

Hannah giggled again. "What do I wear?" Zena shone a torch up and down her form. "Oh I think you are perfect just as you are my dear." With a wave of her hand the little group made their way to the clearing, where before long the heady candles were spreading their aromatic fragrance over the area.

The high priestess stood behind the altar. Facing her were Deana with a tight hold on Madge, and Mandy holding Hannah very lightly, more as guidance than a restraint. Zena raised her arms and began muttering under her breath, barely audible at first, then louder, almost hypnotic, as the smoke wrapped itself like a bandage around the four on the lower level. As their eyes started to water, the image of the leader became misty until all they could see was a green vapour emitting from the altar area and floating, merging with the smoke.

They all started to sway together in time to the chanting, soaking up the green fog until they felt part of it. Madge was relaxed. Maybe the newcomer would take the brunt of Zena's attention tonight. It didn't occur to her in her semi conscious state what her alternative role could be. The two sentinels were only too glad to be of service to their mother figure, knowing it was better to please her and supply her pleasure, than leave her unfulfilled.

Graham was fighting the effects of the aroma and decided to call the standby helper Miri in for a moment to give him chance to regain his control. Instantly they swapped, and he returned to Eden so that he couldn't be observed hovering around the site.

Under the cover of the green mist, Zena approached Madge. The woman was now almost delirious, mumbling, coughing. As the priestess snapped her fingers, Deana and Mandy dragged Madge's form to the altar. They manhandled her onto the table, spread her legs wide, and left her head dangling over the other edge. Then they returned to Hannah and took their places each side of her.

Zena's hands were raised above her head. In the right she held a dagger, in the left a burning candle. Her sacrifice stirred, hardly aware of what was taking place, but with just enough feeling left to experience the excruciating pain which was about to be administered in her final moments on earth. It would have spoiled the Vexon's pleasure if Madge had been totally unconscious; therefore a little reaction was essential.

With a sadistic growl she rammed the candle up between her victims' legs and wallowed at the painful reaction of her discarded object of desire. The scream that left Madge's mouth was soon silenced as the blade descended and slit her throat, the blood dripping to the ground. As the nervous reactions ceased, the lifeless body lay used, discarded.

"It pays not to cross me you pathetic corpse," Zena spat at her remains.

Miri, in the form of Hannah automatically felt the urge to help Madge over during her transition, but had to remain semi drugged and leave the task to another of Marie's helpers. Within seconds one was escorting the woman's ideal away from the scene, comforting her bodiless form to adapt to her new state.

Zargot had been observing these previous moments with extreme delight. What a source of pleasure this Vexon was, and what an idiot to think she controlled the power.

CHAPTER 17

Graham and Jenny were exchanging thoughts. The message had been received that several hybrids had been dispatched to earth but spread across the globe. Zargot had supervised the operation and then left the area. Jenny was a little disappointed, as she had hoped to switch off the power to all the creatures in one go, and with helpers standing by to release the fragmented ideals, she could at least feel the relief which was so long overdue.

But maybe this development could be an advantage. If the evil one was using some of his flock tonight, at least his attention would be drawn away from the space area while he used the hybrids for whatever nasty purpose he had planned.

A quick message to Matthew confirmed the Schynings were ready on full power to blast the electrical systems keeping the creatures charged.

"You had better go back for a while," Jenny indicated towards the earth. Zargot is on site and he won't have been alerted by your presence, as you were here when he arrived. But Miri isn't strong enough for this task for too long."

"Agreed." Instantly Graham took over Hannah's form, releasing the helper to return to Eden until needed. Quickly he surveyed the stage before the effects of the smoky haze dulled his senses.

There before him, merging with the green air he recognized entities from other worlds, floating over the sombre remains of what had once been Madge. Their cackling laughter filled the night as they gloated over the spectacle. But there was something else which held his attention. Zena's eyes were closed as she called in evil spirits to do her bidding, and she seemed unaware of the figure just in front of the altar which Graham recognized immediately. It was one of the hybrids. This meant Zargot was near, for only he could be behind this visitation.

Mandy and Deana seemed barely aware of what was going on around them, but would utter strangled screams as they surfaced in consciousness enough to catch sight of one image or another. So when the hybrid appeared immediately in front of Mandy, raised its thin arm and pointed at her, she fell into a dead faint.

Zargot knew she would remember the incident and dispatched the creature to its next call. There would be many such sightings this night, some would be whispered to a close friend but most keep secret, for the viewers would not wish to explain their whereabouts or their activities.

Graham was fighting to stay alert, knowing how close Zargot was to Hannah's body, and was ready to switch in an instant. But now the evil one seemed centred on Zena who was getting ready to initiate her newly found treasure, and this delight was something in which he must indulge.

Mandy groaned on the ground and slowly pulled herself to her feet as the high priestess snapped her fingers first to her, then Deana. Together they stripped Hannah until she was clad only in her white boots, then they shrank back as their mistress approached.

Fortunately for Graham, Zargot chose this moment to enter the lesbian Vexon's body to savour the entree to his meal before moving on to the main course at a much bigger ritual, and finally the sweet course many earth miles away. But this was certainly a tasty little appetizer and not to be missed.

Zena sensed the power which overwhelmed her being, but mistakenly imagined it was her own. Slowly she glided towards Hannah who in turn raised her arms towards her, the eyes glazed with a distant look of one in a deep trance. Graham had rehearsed this moment carefully, and knew there was a limit to which he could go in response to the advances and a narrow margin in which to tease the evil forces. Outside these bounds he could arouse the suspicion of the more experienced one now occupying the creature in front of him.

Zena clasped the outstretched hands and moved them to her own body, then started to stroke every inch of this new object, so pleasing to her eye. The two other girls now had turned with their backs to the scene, so there was no earthly witness to the events which were about to happen.

Madge's ideal was being comforted following the sudden and traumatic nature of her passing over. She was full of remorse, but realized it was too late to be sorry for getting herself into such a mess. If only she could go back and have another chance, but in the system of things that was rarely allowed. She had only completed three of her earth lives and would have to wait until placed again, which could be anywhere and in any time. That was something over which she would have no control.

Jenny was aware of the transition and feared for Graham's ideal. She knew all along she was playing a dangerous game, which she was prepared to undertake for ever, but when a big operation involved others, she felt a great responsibility for them. This ran deeper than physical safety on earth where one tangible existence could be snuffed out, this covered endless space and never ending time, where the ongoing battle would always rage until evil could be overthrown. But while the opposing forces refused to relent, the war would continue.

Now she prepared to transport to the hybrid holding zone and call in the waiting Schynings to dispose of all the pathetic scraps of Zargot's creation, knowing that any one of them could have been produced from Marie's eggs.

Det.Sgt.Williams drove past the lane leading to the Stokes abode, and noticed Robert's car parked nearby. He felt a slight twinge of relief. Knowing it was now proved that this father had been cleared of the rapes, he knew that if he was visiting, the girls would be safe. But something made him stop his vehicle. What if Bradley was visiting the mother and the girls had gone out? He knew he must have the answer before pursuing his task.

Quickly he parked nearer, and within seconds was making his way to Beth's front door. The excuse he needed soon entered his brain as he gently tapped the door. Beth peered round as she opened it a fraction, but when she recognized Roger, she opened it fully, beckoning him to enter.

"Hello sergeant, what brings you here?" As the small cottage had no hallway, Roger was relieved to see the assembled party obviously at ease watching the television.

"Good news Mrs.Stokes." Roger almost whispered. Then nodding in Robert's direction he added, "Could I have a quick word with you two?"

Robert was already on his feet noticing the smile on the policeman's face. "Kitchen?" He asked Beth.

"Oh yes, of course."

The girls looked up as the three disappeared from view, then immediately turned their attention back to the film which had just got to a critical stage.

"They'll miss the best bit" Lizzie mumbled. "Fancy him coming now can't be that important." As ever she still tried to play down anything that might upset her friend.

"I know" Margaret half replied, equally engrossed.

In the kitchen the sergeant immediately said "I'll come to the point. Two things. Firstly the reports show you are innocent of the rapes Mr. Bradley, thought you'd like to know." Robert turned and hugged Beth, then faced the officer. "But how did you know I was here?"

"That's the second point, quite by chance. I was passing and saw your car, and it gave me a good excuse to see that everything was alright."

"In what way, alright?" Beth frowned.

Roger cast a cautious glance to the door and lowered his voice. "It was a golden opportunity to check that the girls were in, safe you understand."

Robert looked serious now. "What are you saying? Do you know something?"

Williams tried to give a reassuring smile. "I might be on to something, but it's too early to say yet. But could you do me a favour?"

They both nodded and said in unison "Of course."

"In view of my enquiries, could you, between you, make sure that the girls don't go out alone, or are left here alone?"

"Certainly we will," Beth jumped in eagerly, "after the last episode I haven't gone out in the evenings. I've made sure I've visited anybody in the day when the girls are at work."

"Good." Williams gave her a gentle smile, "I would be grateful."

Robert slipped an arm round Beth's shoulder, "You will let us know won't you, when you know more."
"Of course. I'll keep you informed." As he turned to go Beth said "Sergeant, do you know who it could be?"
"Only guess work." was the reply, but Robert was quick to pick up on the hesitation.
"You have somebody in mind don't you? For God's sake man, we have a right to -----"
"You will know soon enough when we have sufficient evidence. Now if you will excuse me."

The girls watched as their parents saw the man out, and smiled as they rejoined them.
"You've missed the end Mum" Lizzie sounded so disappointed.
"It was good "Margaret added, then between them the girls recounted the films final moments. Much went over the heads of the older pair, who both shared mixed feelings. Relief at the forensic results, but added fear that the attacker could be on their doorstep. Somebody known to them. Beth gave a little shudder unnoticed by all but Robert.

Williams headed for the home of Treloar. He was determined to nail this fiend whom he was sure was the one responsible. As the car pulled to a halt opposite the house, the officer cast his eyes to the first floor where the man occupied a flat. All appeared to be in darkness. "Missed him." Roger thought, but then noticed a small glimmer of light flickering from one of the windows. The heavy curtains were closed, but at the top they had not quite met, producing a small V of illumination.

As his eyes became accustomed to the gloom, Roger noticed the beam was not from a light bulb which would be still, not from a television which produced a bluish white light, but a warm glow such as that from a candle. He sat and mused. "Why have a candle burning? His electricity could be off. He liked candles, some people did it seemed. Or he was some kind of religious fanatic who was conducting a mass - ". He stopped in mid thought as the ideal sprang into his brain.
"Black Magic, mixed with rape, with young maidens, hypnotism, it's all falling into place."

Williams didn't yet know just how this man fitted into the jig saw, or if he had any connection with the Mandy lot, but one thing was certain, whatever it was, he was going to get to the bottom of it.

Zena had thoroughly abused the bodily form of Hannah, who still appearing to be tranced had responded in ways which surpassed anything the Vexon had ever known. This creature would be her possession from now on, hers and hers alone, to be untouched by any other person or force. This was what she had been seeking and finally found.

Blood was running down the new victim's legs and into the once white boots, but she seemed unaware of it.

"A virgin," Zena breathed in satisfaction, "the powers commanded by me have sent a virgin."

Zargot left her body with contempt. "You worthless form, you are nothing without me." and he departed to his next prey. She felt the force leave her and sank from exhaustion to her knees, still believing she had summoned the evil spirit, and a little peeved that it had left without her bidding.

Graham immediately called Miri to take over so that he could confirm Zargot's destination, and was relieved to notice that he had not returned to the holding zone. The sexual urges were to the fore of his intentions tonight and he would take over as many mortals as he deemed necessary in order to feed his desire.

CHAPTER 18

The earth visiting hybrids had been programmed to home in on selected sites, then move a few miles away and attack a local landmark with their lasers. This would cause the required diversion needed, and occupy the local peace keeping forces away from planned rituals. Apart from this task, Zargot was thrilled at any wanton destruction in any part of the universe, and if people were injured or killed, so much the better. He had been known to create disasters and sadness just for the sheer joy of it. Hence Jenny's determination to overthrow him.

The British Isles had been targetted for the start of the operation, and as the world revolved, the malice would spread westward across the Atlantic and on towards Haiti. The hybrids should really stir up some beliefs there.

An approaching group of hybrid vessels was picked up on radar of a jet fighter plane which immediately communicated to base. The next moment the jet was blown out of the sky, leaving only the last message as proof of the sighting. Ranks were closed in an instant with instructions that no word must leak concerning the event.

In Ireland, a local lad was walking his girlfriend home when he pointed heavenwards. "Look, a shooting star."

His companion laughed. "That's no star Seamus; it's one of them UFO thingies."

"To be sure, you've an imagination in your head." He laughed as the thing sped out of sight.

"Oh is it now? And where do you suppose it's gone to then?"

More intent on each other than anything extra-terrestrial they made their way home. The girl's mother laughed when they recounted the experience. "Ah to be sure, the loves got to the pair of you. You'll be telling me you've seen little green men next." And so the incident was dismissed.

Many such sightings were noted and when something nearby was set alight, people thought a plane had crashed, until no wreckage was found. Tongues began to wag. Newspapers tried to be first with any new angle on the subject, but most was estimation, not fact.

Mandy had been the only one to see the hybrid at that particular venue, and when she tried to mention it, Zena reprimanded her. If the girl had witnessed something she had missed was bad enough, and the last thing she wanted was for the fact to be bandied about like a huge joke.

Fortunately, the girl seemed vague, and was happy to accept she had merely hallucinated.

"The candles do that." Zena explained as they gathered up the remains of the orgy and prepared to leave. The truth of the happening was beginning to sink in and Deana asked in a weak voice, "What's going to happen to her?" She pointed to Madge's body.

"Nothing." was the reply snapped into the night.

"But we can't just leave her here?" Deana knew this was the wrong thing to say as the words left her mouth.

Zena turned deliberately until her face was inches from the woman. "Are you asking to be next?" The venom of the question almost froze Deana to the ground. She managed a faint "No."

Graham had returned to Hannah's body and was sobbing quietly and shivering. Zena spun round.

"Cover her up," she ordered but as soon as Mandy moved near with the blonds' clothes, she roughly pushed her away saying "I'll do it. Don't you dare touch her. She is mine now. Nobody mauls what belongs to me."

Mandy and Deana were eager to get out of the clearing. Even in the dark, lit only by one torch, they could feel Madge's presence which was unnerving them by the second.

"Can I go home now please?" Graham made the voice pleading knowing this is what the Vexon needed to hear.

"Of course my dear." But to the other two, "come on, get a move on."

It was a weary but mixed little band that found its way back to the car. Zena was still on a high plain having been fully satisfied, but eagerly awaiting the next time, and also jubilant in her successful summoning of the spirits to assist her. She felt power in her hands, her mind, and her being as a whole. Mandy could still see the hybrid's eye slits before her face, and Deana was overcome with the unexpected death, the blood of which was on all their hands. Graham knew his task was almost over and called Miri back to give him chance to get a current placing on the evil master. Satisfied as to his whereabouts, Graham took over Hannah's form for the last time, as he needed to be in charge at the parting.

If Det.Sgt.Williams could have witnessed the car leaving the field track that night, he would have had much to report to his superior, and little did he know, as he tracked down Vernon Treloar, that the body of Bradley's wife now lay abandoned, waiting to be found.

Zena was insistent that Hannah could be contacted for future meetings and noted that she was staying at the Bay Tree Hotel, or so she believed.

"I'm only staying for a while," Graham whispered as he climbed out of the car.

"We'll see," Zena gave her a knowing smile, determined not to loose this one.

"You certainly won't see" Graham thought as he took the side path and disappeared from view.

Marie was feeding back to Jenny up to the minute information of Zargot's movements. Graham had done a fine job keeping him well and truly occupied in one place for as long as possible leaving the way clear for the massive hybrid shut down. Knowing delay could have disastrous results and thwart the operation; Jenny wasted no time and switched to the holding area. She quickly scanned the hybrids, noting the J1-6 ones were missing, and assumed they were out on a chosen mission.

She sent the attack order to Matthew who arrived with the first wave of Schyning light panels, all fully charged. Systematically they traversed the rows, blowing the power on each section. It was agreed not to do the lot in one go, as the sudden shut down may alert either a sentinel, or the master himself. They were about half way through when Marie's urgent thought warning came through.

"He's on the move again."

In a flash, the working party evacuated the area, and held off at a safe distance until the all clear was given. Satisfied the evil one was indulging his desires again, they ventured back and continued the task. Helpers were already clearing the fragments in transition, and Jenny felt deep sadness that they should finish an existence this way, and regretted she couldn't have intervened sooner.

One thing niggling at her was the current position of the J hybrids. It had become common knowledge that, even though these had been adjusted by Johhahn, they still had extra evil directions which could be put to good use by the master. In his hands there was no limit to the destruction which could follow. So where were they tonight?

Unbeknown to either power, the six could merge as ordinary hybrids, and transform themselves as required. They were becoming an independent source of malice. They hung undetected in the last hundred specimens to be terminated, gradually moving their position until they were the very last ones who would receive the power loss.

Jenny was gratified to have released so many, but still felt very cautious about the operation. Suddenly, to everyone's amazement she ordered an immediate complete withdrawal.

"What's wrong?" Matthew was the first to enquire.

"Don't know. But something is."

The Schynings communicated with them, begging to finish the job quickly, but Jenny held them back.

"It's been too easy. We should have been intercepted by now, even from an ultimate from one of the Zarg spirals."

Marie picked up the thought wave and joined them. "They're too busy arguing about some power struggle. Think they're taking advantage of the cat being away."

"That follows." Jenny still mused. "And Zargot? Where is he now?"

"Think he is hovering over a few different covens on the coast of New Jersey, picking the best, Graham's keeping him in view."

"Well that's something." Jenny still did not give the order to return. The Schynings' power had been used considerably, and Jenny felt they could be overcome should anything tax them further.

"When are your reinforcements due?" she directed the question to their leading light panel.
"Not for an earth quarter hour, but we have sufficient power to finish the remainder."
"I'm not so sure." Jenny still held off. Her instinct warned her that all was not well.
"I'll see how many are left. All wait here." She did a double switch, and instantly reported "Eighty five." After a moment she directed "Go in and take ten then return."

Immediately the light panels zoomed into the holding zone, switched off the ten and were back.
"No problem" they confirmed. Jenny double switched again.
"Next ten." She indicated, and on the Schynings' return thought, "only sixty five more."

Matthew was still bemused. "Why the slowing up Jenny?"
"Because of all the sightings reports we've had back from the earth area, all the hybrids have been the same."
Matthew gleaned the problem "And you want to know where the six specials are."
"Precisely. If they are not on earth, and they are not at any other location, where else are they?"

A stunned pause covered the group, as they all realized why Jenny was so good at masterminding the evil leader.
Matthew voiced the feelings of them all." You suspect they are here?"
"Where else? That's why we will have to flush them out." Slight anger rose through her being as she thought forcibly "No wonder he is content to roam. He thinks this is guarded."
"But why can't you spot them?" Matthew still did not quite understand how she could be fooled so easily.
"I believe they have taken the appearance of the ordinary ones"
Even the Schynings shuffled uneasily, now realizing the dangerous game they had undertaken.

"Another ten?" Jenny asked. Without a reply they were gone, did the deed and returned. This time everyone was counting down.
"Fifty-five." The tension was mounting by the second. Jenny hoped the electrical energy of her helpers would last. She sent them another three times, and at a remainder of twenty five hybrids she called a halt.

"Now what?" Matthew wondered. He was answered by Jenny switching to the zone for several moments and on her return, all the assembled party waited for her to communicate.

"I believe them to be there. But it will take more power than we have. I think they will retaliate, and I don't know what I'm up against, as I have no way of knowing their full potential."

The Schynings asked to take out more in the meantime, but were refused. "Too dangerous." Jenny imparted. "We've been on borrowed time. They could be anywhere." She thanked the visitors gratefully, and dispatched them, saying she would wait for the new group as she needed their fully charged power. She then prepared herself inwardly for the coming onslaught.

Vernon Treloar, now in desperate need of taking Lizzie at the first opportunity, was becoming almost careless, as the urge placed in him by Zargot, was driving him to distraction. The craving was like a drug which he must have at all costs.

He prepared himself to go out, not as Vedron, but as himself, concocting a tale that Lizzie was needed urgently at the nursing home. Being the kind hearted girl that she was, he estimated she would leave her home willingly and go with him. With a little hypnotism, he could get her to forget the subsequent happenings, and return home in a dazed state. If he confirmed she had been alright when he left her, it would be presumed that she had been assaulted afterwards, thus freeing him of any suspicion.

It was so clever, it couldn't fail. Feeling very pleased with himself, and anticipating the forthcoming relief, he set off on his bike in the direction of Lizzie's home.

It therefore came as a shock when he saw Robert's car parked near the lane leading to the cottage. This was something he had not envisaged. But did it matter? He got off his bike and paused. If he asked Lizzie to go to the nursing home, maybe Mr. Bradley would offer a lift, or at least want to see her safely home again, in view of her recent experiences. The longing ache in his body made him fidget, not knowing how to contain himself.

He was so overwhelmed with the need in his lower parts, he did not notice the car which had pulled up across the street, and parked quietly, its lights off. So when the Vexon reluctantly left, his mission abandoned, he was carefully observed by Det.Sgt.Williams. Another tiny piece of the jig saw in place.

"A cup of tea before you go Robert?" Beth got up as the programme finished, and smiled at the relaxed form of her friend sprawled in the easy chair. The girls nudged each other as he looked up sleepily, but rather lovingly at Lizzie's Mum.

"A strong coffee might be better. It's only a short drive but I could do with feeling more awake than I do at present."

"Pity he has to go, isn't it Mum?" Lizzie tilted her head, a saucy little expression creeping across her face.

"That will do from you miss," her mother pretended to scold, but the atmosphere was so easy and friendly, nothing could have spoiled it for any of them.

Robert stretched, wishing more than ever he could stay with his beloved Beth, but his mind turned to Madge.

"I'd better get back," he looked at Margaret, "your Mother will be coming home about now, I suppose." His daughter's reply was a disinterested shrug. There was no love lost there, and she didn't care what the woman was doing, as long as she didn't have to see her.

Beth came in from the kitchen with a tray and handed a coffee to Robert.

"You two can have cocoa, calm you down a bit," she grinned at the girls.

"Thanks Mum." "Thanks Auntie Beth." The two chorused together making both parents laugh.

Finishing his drink, Robert took his leave of the three ladies, and was soon heading back to his home, wondering if Madge would be there already, and if so, in what state. If she wasn't there, would he wait up? "No" he decided firmly. She had been coming in later and later, and the mere sight of her made him feel sick. He even wondered just what he had ever seen in her.

He pulled into the drive and switched off the engine. A quick glance told him the place was in total darkness which meant she could be in bed, or may not even be back. Being in no hurry to find out, he checked his watch as the security light clicked on. Eleven-fifteen.

It was almost a relief as he checked the house and found it empty. If he hurried, he could be in bed, in his own room, before she returned. That would save him the sight of the hussy, and mean that he need not speak to her until the next morning. By then, tonight would only be a blur to her, and that would be the end of the matter.

"The end of it" he thought as he cleaned his teeth "what will happen? She can't go on like this, and nor can I". More than ever now, after the peaceful evening which was still wafting over him like a soothing breeze, he wanted his beloved Beth, added to which the two girls would make a perfect family. He shook himself out of his mused state, and quickly got into bed and put out the light.

"Come in when you like, and how you like," he muttered to himself, "I don't care."

CHAPTER 19

The new batch of Schynings had arrived all fully charged, and increased in numbers at the message relayed by the departing troupe.

Quickly Jenny ordered "There are twenty-five hybrids still to take out. But we cannot take any risks. Use full power on each. The lesser ones will turn off quickly, and then move on." She warned them about the six J's and the dangerous mission her supporters were facing. In view of Jenny's previous help to their race, they deemed it an honour to be of service to her now, both to help release the trapped souls, and get even with Zargot.

Leaving Marie in command, Jenny accompanied the light panels and spheres on this final attack. As they reached the holding area, only nineteen scraps were left hanging in position.

"Take them out." she commanded the Schynings, but at the same time she scanned the area for the other six which could only be the J1-6.

In a flash the nineteen ideals were gathered up by helpers and released from their mental living tombs.

Jenny knew the others had not departed, they had to be somewhere, but where? She switched to the departure area. Empty. All the craft were out, covering the earth locations on the master's instructions. This caused her to note that the returning creatures still had to be released at a later time.

Without warning, she felt a surge of power from behind her ideal. The six J's were approaching her in a combined mass appearing as one form, yet still showing all six pairs of eyes, wide now with no hint of the slits they had assumed before.

She was no stranger to the evil of Zargot, but she had never known anything quite like the venomous force which was emitting from the thing approaching. But these creatures, which Johhahn had programmed, were not aware of Jenny's endless surprises. As well as being the only ultimate to perform the double switch, she had perfected another little trick on her return to power. This seemed a good time to try it out.

Carefully positioning herself near the edge of the departure well, a drop of at least twenty feet, she faced the being as it gathered speed to attack. At the moment of impact, she split her ideal, separating it for the hybrids to pass through, and rejoining immediately.

The combined thing, caught off guard descended into the pit. "Get it" she called to the Schynings who, from above, directed all the power available at the creature. It let out the most hideous scream as it writhed helpless below them, the electrical charges penetrating it's every inch until it became blackened and scorched beyond return.

As Jenny dismissed the work force, she still felt a slight pang for the remains lying there smoldering, knowing that once part of it had been nurtured from a human source. She returned to where Marie and the Schynings were eagerly waiting, but as they all expressed the relief at the destruction of such an entity, Jenny stopped.

"What is it?" Marie was surprised at her leader's lack of jubilation.

"Notice anything? Or rather the lack of it?" Jenny's attention was drawn back to the area they had just left.

Marie was quick to join her apprehension. "The helpers. Where are the helpers?" As with the ordinary hybrids, Marie had placed some of her most reliable prefects ready for the transition of the ideals at the point of death, if that's what you could call it. There were six highly experienced ones ready to take the J's occupants over. But up to now they hadn't returned.

This could only mean one thing. The J's had not been released, and were still in existence. Marie wondered "What if they had already gone, if these had ousted the last human fragments," but then she added "I would have known, I've been carefully monitoring this. No they can't have gone."

Satisfied at her friend's diligence, Jenny decided to descend again to view the situation.

Matthew realized that many light spheres and panels had used most of their energy and he returned them to Schyn, leaving a little band still on hand if required. He was satisfied with their part in the operation and now was patrolling the area to warn of impending danger, leaving his leader free to use Marie as support for the job in hand.

He watched as they both switched to the pit bottom. The sight that met them would have sickened the hardest being in the universe, and even these two stalwarts from Eden shuddered mentally as they joined the waiting helpers.

There, trying to escape from the burnt remains of the J hybrids, were six distorted ideals, struggling madly to extract themselves from the charred mess, but each time a strand emerged it was sucked back. The helpers were grabbing at any slightest tangible part but were being repelled by the unseen evil force which now threatened to absorb them into it.

Jenny indicated for them all to retreat while they could, then switched them back to where Matthew and the remaining Schynings were anxiously waiting.

"What's happening" one of the helpers asked as soon as they were clear. There was a pause as Jenny and Marie exchanged thoughts, and when the explanation was delivered, a strange silence fell over the assembled party.

It was a few moments before anyone communicated.

"So they are trapped," a weak thought emerged from another helper.

Marie noticed Jenny was in deep concentration so offered the reply for her. "The best way to think of it is that if they were on a planet, say earth, they would be classed as earthbound spirits."

"Ghosts?" One of the others cut in. "That's what earth dwellers call them isn't it?"

"In a way." Marie tried to make this as pleasant as possible. "But in this instance, it's not of their own doing."

"Stay here" Jenny's order interrupted them, and she was gone.

Marie continued. "When someone dies on earth or any of the inhabited planets, if they are not at peace, or feel there is something unfinished, they cannot return to Eden, or whatever source, until their ideal will release them. It is a self-entrapment. "

"So they keep themselves there?" The Schynings added.

"Exactly. But this is not one of those cases. These poor things are being held by the evil force that created them." Then after a moment "Unfortunately, we've come across it before."

Jenny's return alerted them. "Almost right Marie?"
"Why, isn't it like the Heraldi asteroid lot?"
"No. I don't think it is an individual's work. Johhahn was a schemer, but he couldn't have produced such a concentration of evil to hold such a number." Jenny scanned the area and continued. "If he had been that good, he would be here now, and not banished to some black hole. No, it's bigger." Again she surveyed the area.
"What is it?" Marie wondered.
"Matthew, could you locate Graham and bring him in" It was not a request and Matthew switched to scan the globe.

Jenny moved Marie away from the others and said "I've requested one of the upper spiral to sweep up, follow Zargot's trail and close as many portals as possible. Marie felt a surge of apprehension encompass her.
"You think it's him. No. You know it is. Do you think he's going to pull this thing" she indicated down to the holding zone "whatever it is now, down through one of the portals?"
"I'm not taking the chance." Jenny thought to her friend. "But I think only He can be behind it. Only He is evil enough." They returned to the group.

She thanked the Schynings for their assistance and they all left, leaving the occupants of Eden surveying the tragic area from a distance. There was no point keeping the helpers, as they could be used elsewhere and were always needed somewhere.

So Jenny and Marie awaited the return of Matthew with Graham, when they would all return to Eden to discuss the next vital move.

Vernon Treloar had no choice but to return to his flat, hopelessly deflated at the failure of his mission. No doubt he could have found another target, but to a Vexon, possession was one of the most important traits. And Lizzie was his. Nobody else would do, not even that pathetic friend of hers. Only Lizzie.

Somehow he had acquired a photo of her and he stood naked, staring at the image of his love his juices oozing from him, the saliva trickling from his mouth as he savoured the eyes looking back at him, the slight pouty mouth and the total look of innocence which dominated her features. He must make plans to have her, no matter what, but for now his body must release what it could no longer contain, and as it gushed from him, he sank sobbing to the floor, partly from relief, but mainly from regret that he had wasted what should have been hers.

Roger Williams had followed at a safe distance, and supervised the return of this man, whom he now somehow knew was the one he must ensnare.

But he would have to be satisfied for tonight, and tomorrow he would examine the area of the Carterton road in the hopes of finding new evidence. Whether it would be connected to the female lot in the area, or whether it would be one of Treloar's haunts would remain to be seen.

He prayed it would be the latter, for although it would certainly be a feather in his cap to track down the Mandy group, he had his teeth into getting the handyman, before suspicions were raised and thereby thwart the whole operation.

As he drove home, he pondered over what he may find. Firstly he must find an opening in the hedge bordering the fields, and then find tracks leading to an area which could conceal any sort of ritual or happening. He should ask the farmer's permission, but as he didn't want to raise any undue attention, he decided to see how far he could go undetected.

But that was tomorrow.

The hybrids were performing to perfection, and Zargot was pleased. Under cover of his little 'friends' he could spread wanton destruction wherever he chose. The earth ventures were almost like a dress rehearsal for bigger things to come in the cosmos.

During the pleasures of this night, he had used the creatures to project their image in holographic form, without them leaving their craft. This is what Mandy had encountered, although in the state she was in, had not fathomed how the thing could have appeared and disappeared so quickly. The evil one was careful about the sightings, using only situations that could not be confirmed or verified, where the participants would not wish to be identified.

He was now in Haiti where the natives were performing strange dances and chanting. Here he could really excel, for they would believe anything out of fear for their safety. If any were brave enough not to partake in the rituals, he would instruct a 'friend' to direct a beam at one of the dwellings where it ignited as if my magic.

He found this exhilarating, and tended to overdo the procedure giving the impression the gods were displeased. So intent was he in the success of this added power, he gave little mind to the holding zone, which played straight into Jenny's hands, to a point. There were still the hundred or so hybrids still to return to base, plus the remains of the combined J group entrapping the ideals within.

As soon as Jenny had dispatched the Schynings, she regretted the action and sent Matthew immediately to recall a fully charged group. If the earth visiting creatures had been busy, they would be returning on low power to be recharged. If they could be picked off in mid journey, the surprise element would be on her side, and with them being at a low ebb, it shouldn't take too much power to take them all in one go. She called on Marie to bring in more helpers to see over the group in transition when needed. They would all relax a little if the task could be completed to this point, the only remaining problem being the charred mass still lying in the pit.

It was Saturday morning, a crisp day towards the end of October, and the sun picked its way into the room where Robert Bradley lay. He stretched, yawned and looked at the clock. Seven thirty. Last night still lingered in his mind like a friend not wanting to leave. Slowly reality crept back into his brain.

"Madge" he thought reluctantly"I suppose she's back." Without any hurry he went to the toilet, then slowly made his way into the room they had both shared for so long. He peeped round the door. If she was asleep he certainly had no intention of waking her.

The sight of the unused bed hit him. This was a first. She had been late in before, but had always returned at some time during the night, from where he didn't know. But this. He felt a slight pang of concern, not from love, more from wondering where she could have got to, and he supposed he should know if she was alright.

He went downstairs, put the kettle on, and while he was waiting for it to boil, he went to the phone in the hall. He picked up the receiver to call Beth, thought for a moment, then replaced it. He shouldn't bother her, not yet. What could he say, only that Madge hadn't come home.
"Too early to disturb her anyway," he muttered to himself and went back to the kitchen to make the tea.

The feelings that raced through him were more of anger than concern. He knew the woman had been up to something for weeks. She had cut him and Margaret out of her life not divulging any of her outings, or people she was meeting. It had been quite a relief to him, especially when Beth had taken in his daughter. He knew the girl would have more love from her than she ever knew from her own mother, plus it had given him more chances to see the love of his dreams.

But the change in his wife recently was certainly not a pleasant one. Not only had she altered her appearance, but her whole attitude had soured.
"She's done this deliberately," he seethed," she knew where I was going last night, and she's trying to get back at me. Well it won't work."

He drank his tea, looked again at his watch, and decided he must talk to someone. It was just gone eight o'clock, he would ring Beth.

A sleepy voice answered. "Hello. Oh hello Uncle Robert, I'll get Mum." Lizzie handed the phone to her mother who had appeared at her side.
"This is a nice surprise Robert, is everything alright?"
"I'm not sure. Look, I'm sorry to ring you so early but---"
"No, no that's OK, what is it?" She looked at Lizzie who was hovering.
"It's alright dear." She waited for Lizzie to disappear into the kitchen before continuing.
"Go on."
"Beth, Madge hasn't come home yet."
"What" she almost shouted, then quickly lowered her voice to a whisper.
"You mean she's been out all night?"
"That's exactly what I mean. Where in God's name can the woman be?"
"Have you told the police?"

"No, not yet. What can they do? Oh God, haven't we had enough of the police breathing down our necks without her doing something to draw all the more attention to us." He was still angry, and was shouting.
"Look, calm down Robert. We don't know that she hasn't just stayed with a friend or something. Perhaps you should give it a bit longer."
Lizzie came back from the kitchen. "What's up?"
Beth asked Robert to wait a moment as she turned to the girl and said "It's nothing much dear, Madge stayed out all night, but I'm sure everything's going to be alright, so best not bother Margaret yet eh?"
Lizzie nodded and made her way back upstairs with two cups of tea.
"Sorry about that, thought I'd better tell her now, she'll be good with Margaret, very protective you know."
"Yes, thanks. Beth. I'm sorry, I shouldn't have sounded off, it's just - well with everything."
Beth's soothing voice floated down the line "You don't have to explain." Then after a slight pause. "What will you do? I mean how long will you give her before - ?"
He finished the sentence for her "Before I call the police. Oh I don't know. The thing is I've no idea where she could be. I don't know who to ring. I don't know who she sees."
"Well I'll be here. Let me know the moment she comes back."
"I will. And thanks a million Beth."

They said their farewells and the first call of many that day was ended.

CHAPTER 20

"Yes, I'm just off now, I thought I'd make an early start." Det. Sgt. Williams was glad his chief had called. "Bye the way" he sipped at his tea between phrases, "when you circled that patch of road, you didn't actually say which side was the one I'm to look at." Jones confirmed it as being the left hand side going from Burford then hung up.

The sergeant gathered his things together thinking, "It's funny, when somebody knows a fact, they think everyone else does as well." He stopped and mused for a moment. Now that's a useful angle. Feeling thwarted that last nights stalking had produced little, he set off in high spirits feeling that if he only looked hard enough, a few answers would be there for him to find.

As he drove, his mind churned over the various evidence, from Barry Timms' statement, making him wonder where the Mandy element fitted in, to the rapes and attacks in the area, and most of all he kept coming back to Vernon Treloar.

The traffic was light on the Carterton road, and Roger decided to park on the opposite side, in every gateway if necessary, and view the area from that angle. After all, the reports had come in from couples parked out of the way but with a view of any track or break in the hedgerow.

The first two proved useless. There were no gaps, no surface where any vehicle could have been driven. He began to wonder if the reports had been correct. Maybe at night people had got their bearings wrong, or even changed them to cover their own misdoings.

Checking the road was clear, he moved along to the next gate. This was set next to a couple of trees which afforded more shelter than the previous field entrances. He stopped, reversed and switched off the engine. Again he scanned the landscape. As he got out of the car he noticed tracks at his feet. So maybe somebody had been parked here recently. The marks were too narrow for farm vehicles and his spirits rose a little. To the left his vision was met with the same unbroken view, but as his eyes roved to the right he saw an indentation in the grass verge.

He crossed the road and followed the grass until he came to the depression. There was a very narrow opening. From the angle of approach it was invisible and even to anyone coming the other way, Roger figured you would have to know it was there or it would be missed. There was no gate and the field appeared to have been left fallow this year, and not visited regularly. What a marvellous hiding place.

A few steps off the grass led him onto the rough track which he noticed bore car tyre marks. The elation welled in his veins as he felt himself being drawn nearer to the answers he was seeking. He wished Jones had been here to witness this, but he could always come down at a minutes notice if something tangible was discovered.

He stooped and gently touched the soil. It was just tacky enough to hold the tread marks, but a little dry dust had been spread to the sides with the movement of vehicles. Taking a sample packet from his pocket, he carefully scooped up a little of the dirt and sealed it, marking the packet, and returning it to his coat.

Then he viewed the extent of the track. To his left was a fairly high hedge, and to his right the field stretched away unused. Ahead he made out a small group of trees which he estimated to be two hundred yards or more away. He imagined them to be in a dip judging from the position of the branches and the height. All this he took in with a single glance, and as he stood just inside the field he felt more than heard, the stillness, the quietness which seemed to be enveloping him.

The detective had seen many unpleasant sights during his career, but the feeling engulfing him at this moment was nothing like anything he had ever experienced. Something was pushing him back, forcing him to venture no further, and it took all his will power to resist and stand his ground. Eventually, he returned to his car, and as the power released him, he felt his skin break out into a cold sweat.

At that moment, he knew he could not investigate further without his superior being there. He didn't care how it would sound as he related the overwhelming instinct to turn and run. Surely the chief would realize they were on the brink of discovering the truth. But whatever he was about to find out, he was certainly not going to do it alone, not there.

"It's true." Matthew and Graham were reporting to Jenny that only half the expected hybrids were returning to their base.

Jenny beckoned mentally to Marie. "Quick let's take those without delay." Then to the two messengers, "We must know where the others are. This operation has gone well in some ways; I want to complete it as much as possible."

As they left she imparted, "We will be at the holding zone." Marie soon located the Schynings, a small group but all fully charged and ready for action. It wasn't long before the first returning craft appeared. Jenny let them enter the transportation area then ordered their demise. She was careful to keep the workers far enough away from the evil mass, still in the bottom of the well, in case its power pulled them in. Before long, about fifty hybrids had been released, the helpers carefully taking the long suffering ideals away.

Once again Jenny thanked the Schynings for their help, but confirmed that, until they had located the remaining group, she would need them no more at the moment, and they departed.

Soon Matthew and Graham joined them and the four switched to Eden for discussion of the events to date. What they had to impart brought more apprehension to the daughter of the Almighty One. It appeared that Zargot, temporarily satisfied with the games of the night, had moved the hybrids to an area away from the earth, where they appeared to be stationery, with no apparent purpose.

"And they are doing nothing?" Jenny was puzzled. What was her arch enemy planning now?

"Seems not," Graham thought, "they do seem to be massing, but we couldn't work out why."

"Give me the exact location." Jenny absorbed the area and switched there, pausing only to check the numbers before returning.

"Well," Marie was anxious, "was He there?"

"Not at that precise moment, but he is supervising the operation. I left as he was bringing in the next lot. I think they are all there now."

"Did he notice you?" Marie was still concerned, knowing the battle which was imminent.

"Wouldn't think so."
"Are you thinking of taking them out where they are?" Graham wondered.
Jenny pondered for a second before replying. "I think this is something big" she was very slow in her thought, "he is positioning them half way between the earth and the moon."
Matthew was still bewildered. "But why? Perhaps they are waiting to attack again."
"No." Jenny churned the location and distance through her very self. "Whatever it is, it will be executed from there." She did a double switch. "I don't like it."
The others waited for her to be more specific, so she explained. "It isn't directed at the earth. They are all facing away from the planet."
Marie ventured "You mean, towards the moon?"
Jenny realized they needed to know as much as she did. "To where the moon will be. Graham, take a quick look at the moon's surface, the part that always faces earth. Do a scan. Be quick." Needed no further encouragement he was gone.

Nothing more was exchanged until his return.

Mandy and Deana had both woken on the morning following the ritual with heavy heads, and what felt like a tremendous hang over. But worse than any physical feeling, was an overwhelming sense of guilt and fear.

Deana wanted to be rid of Zena's clutches, but after witnessing, albeit in a drugged state, the events surrounded Madge's death, she knew that for her to cross this high priestess as she called herself would be fatal. That is unless she got in first. That would be the only release she and her friend could ever hope for. She made up her mind to ring Mandy as soon as the room stopped spinning.

The sight of the alien was still in front of the other girl's face. She could not get away from it, even with closed eyes, it was there staring at her, pointing. She wondered if she had imagined the slaughter of their companion, but as reality slowly crept back into her body, she knew with absolute horror that it was no figment, but the horrible truth. She also made up her mind to make a phone call, but not to Deana. She was going to make an anonymous call to the police.

Zena must have been the only one satisfied and refreshed and waiting for the next session. Her disgusting treatment whilst slaying Madge only fuelled her pleasure in taking the new creature, Hannah, and what a delight she had turned out to be. The best yet. She must have her again, soon. She felt like the spider spinning its web, little realizing that she could soon become the fly ensnared in her own net.

Beth was on edge. Surely Madge must have returned by now, but if so, why hadn't Robert rung her. Not being able to stand the suspense any longer, she made her way to the phone and was about to pick it up when it rang. Grabbing the receiver she almost shouted "Yes?" praying it would be his voice.

"Beth, she's still not back. It's nearly eleven, what should I do?" The strain of waiting was echoed in his question.

"I don't know. I feel the same as you, about the police, I mean." She was in no hurry for him to report the matter, but at the same time was worried as to what had happened. Searching for an alternative she offered "Robert, I know this might sound silly, but she couldn't have left you could she?"

"I must admit, the thought crossed my mind, but she hasn't taken any clothes." He felt like adding "More's the pity," but until he knew the reason for her disappearance, he decided it best not to utter such things.

"I don't know what to say Robert."

After a few moments of small talk he said. "It's no good. I'm going to have to report it, whatever they think."

"Are you sure?" Beth still wasn't happy with the situation.

"Look, I'll try and get hold of that Williams chap, he seemed to believe me." He felt that was a good idea but Beth hesitated.

"Maybe, if you just reported her as a missing person, to anyone, they might not tie it up straight away. You know, just log the report."

"Beth you're wonderful. I'll do that."

With a few short goodbyes he rang off.

Robert Bradley was trying to stay calm. With the detective thankfully not available, he was having to deal with a very slow speaking old plodder who seemed to be the only officer on duty. The

man on the end of the phone didn't seem at all concerned about the fact that Madge was missing.
"You see sir, she's not a minor, or mentally handicapped or anything like that. There's not much we can do. She has the right to please herself, and if she has chosen to go off for a while, that's up to her."
"But surely you could make enquiries?"
The policeman took a breath. "Look sir, if you wanted a bit of peace and quite, or a break from it all, you wouldn't thank us for sticking our noses in and chasing after you, would you? You see sir, an adult has the right of freedom. You'd be surprised the things we hear and see. Happens all the time. You mark my words, she'll be back. When she's ready that is."

Robert realized this was going nowhere, but he made the man promise he would at least make a note of the fact, although he imagined it would find the waste paper basket as soon as the phone was put down.

So before he rang off, he informed the officer that he would be in touch again, with his superior if necessary if his wife did not return.

As he replaced the receiver with a crash he couldn't help balancing the irony of it all. When he needed the police, they weren't interested, but when they wanted him, that was different. Then they came crawling out of the woodwork.

Beth had agreed with her friend that she tell both the girls the current situation, and when she felt ready, called them both to sit in the lounge. Lizzie broke the ice a little by asking straight away "Is Margaret's Mum alright?"
"Why shouldn't she be ?"Margaret's question bore no tone of concern, and both the others looked at her strangely.
"Um -" Beth began, "well Margaret, it seems, from your father that is, that your mother went out last night ---"
"Tell us something new." Margaret huddled into the settee and again Lizzie looked at her in bewilderment.
"The thing is, darling," Beth wasn't sure what the next reaction would be, "she hasn't come home yet, that is, she stayed out all night."
"Good, give my dad some peace."
"Margaret!" Lizzie and her mother chorused, but it was the girl who continued.

"Aren't you the least bit bothered. Aren't you worried in case something dreadful has happened?" For once she lost her protectiveness which always dominated her, and was now in full flow of utter surprise.

The violent reaction which followed shook Beth rigid. Margaret rose to her feet, her eyes blazing and her hands clenched until the knuckles were white as she hissed through clenched teeth, "After the life she has given me, after the way she's treated my dad, you think I have an ounce of love or respect for her? Well let me tell you now, I hope she is dead." The tears were starting to ooze from the eyelids and trickle down the flushed face. As she turned to rush upstairs, she yelled again "I hope the evil bitch is dead, dead, dead."

Lizzie made to follow her but Beth stopped her in mid track. "Leave her for a while dear. Let her calm down."

Her daughter sank to the chair sobbing now. "I've never seen her like that Mum, she's always been so - what's the word?"

"I think you mean withdrawn, into herself."

Lizzie nodded. "That's it. I wouldn't have believed she'd got a harsh word in her, let alone that."

Beth slipped her arm round her, loving her for her caring ways, but knowing she lacked the worldly experience to help her understand. She slowly stroked her hair.

"People do funny things sometimes. Things we don't know why, but there's always a reason for them."

"Do you think it's got something to do with when she was attacked?" Lizzie sniffed and looked up at her mum.

"Could very well have. You see, you were able to talk to me when - when it happened, but poor Margaret had to keep it all locked up inside. She couldn't have discussed it with Madge, could she now?"

"Oh no." The horror showed instantly on the innocent face. "She would have said it was dirty. I think she called her some horrible names anyway."

"So you see, this is probably only a way of releasing all those pent up emotions, and most likely going back over many years, all her life in fact."

The mother got up and said "Tell you what, pop the kettle on, and I'll go and see if she's alright now." Glad of feeling useful, Lizzie willingly did as she was asked, grateful that she had such an understanding parent.

"Can I come in?" Beth gently tapped the bedroom door.
"I suppose so," was the reply. As the woman entered the room she was astounded at the sight which met her eyes. The room was strewn with clothes, belongings, make up, as though someone had rampaged through it. In the middle of the mess sat Margaret, hatred pouring out of her as she stared at Beth with hostility.

Lizzie's mum stood transfixed with horror and bewilderment, unable to speak. Before she could draw breath the girl got to her feet.
"You are all liars. You've all being lying to me. Did you think I was so stupid not to know what you were doing?
"MARGARET." Beth's tone was sharp, and it took all her presence of mind to stay in control. "Margaret," she said again, quieter now "I will tell you anything you want to know."
The girl's head went to one side. "How can I trust you?"

Beth made her way through the mess to the bed and sat down, indicating her to sit by her side. Very slowly and with great distrust Margaret sat on the bed but well away eyeing her opponent as though she was about to be attacked.

Deliberately the older woman explained about both suspected rapes and Madge's treatment of her, following by explaining why she had brought her to live with them. At this point she included Lizzie's protectiveness.
"Don't you see dear, we wanted you here because we love you, Lizzie adores you, she doesn't want you to be upset."
"So why didn't somebody have the decency to tell me all this before. Did you all think I was an imbecile or something?"
"I suppose this had to come out in some form sometime," Beth comforted herself with the thought. There was silence for a moment then she said almost in a whisper "You blame your mother for a lot, don't you?"
"No." was the equally quiet reply. "I blame her for everything."

Beth felt it fitting to let the girl know everything now so that they could all speak freely in future, so she explained the second attack on Lizzie. It appeared to float over Margaret's head and she just shrugged, but suddenly she froze.

"What is it dear?" Beth put out her hand but Margaret jumped up and away from her, her arm extended, pointing accusingly.

"You - you --know him and you won't say who he is." She was becoming hysterical again as something unlocked in her mind.

"Who? That's just it Margaret. We don't know who. That's what your dad is trying to find out. We don't know."

Margaret was shaking, her face white and drawn as the words came out barely audible. "I know I recognized him, so did Liz, but he sent us to sleep, and now I can't remember. But she knows him, she knows him."

"All right dear." Beth now held the shaking form trying to calm her, wondering if she had done the right thing in telling her so much. She would call the doctor to check her over and probably give her something to calm her.

Lizzie had been about to enter the room but stopped as she witnessed the outpouring. She turned, made her way to her own room and fell on her bed sobbing.

CHAPTER 21

Roger Williams strode into the police station heading for the office. He needed a coffee, a very strong one. The duty constable tried to tell him something but the detective held up his hand as he hurried past. "In a minute Jack. I'm sure it can wait."

Unperturbed the uniformed man followed him. "Let me tell you, then you decide."

Knowing he would get no peace until he listened, Roger perched on the edge of the desk and said curtly "Go on then, you probably won't rest until I've heard it."

Very deliberately the officer said, "I know you've been doing some special poking around lately, which is why I think you'll be interested in two phone calls I've had this morning." Roger took a breath. "Go on then."

"Firstly I had a chap on, reporting his wife had been out all night and hadn't returned. Didn't think much of it then." He paused; mostly to make sure he had the other man's full attention before continuing.

"But then I had a call from a young woman, sounded really distressed she did, wouldn't give a name, sounded drunk in fact."

Roger shifted wishing the man would get to the point. "And?"

She said that somebody had been killed last night, at a black magic meeting, and that if she was caught telling us, the same thing would happen to her."

Roger was no longer impatient but piecing together every scrap as it was spread before him. "Her name man, who was it?"

"She wouldn't give it. She just kept saying that she, whoever it was, had killed her, whoever that was. I know it sounds patchy, but I just wondered if it could be the woman reported missing."

Jumping to his feet Roger asked "You didn't say who was missing" As he received the reply his blood ran cold.

"Oh sorry, "the constable flicked through the book he had brought with him, "here we are, her name is Madge Bradley. Reported by her husband, ---"

"Robert Bradley" the sergeant finished for him. He quickly thanked then dismissed the man so that he could phone Det.Ch.Insp.Jones.

As he waited for his senior to answer, the events spun before him as he tried to get everything into perspective.

"Hello Roger, what have you found out?" The voice brought him back.

"A lot. Can you come down?"

He didn't expect a negative answer and was somewhat surprised when Jones said "A bit difficult today, got something big going on here. Tell me what you know and I'll get down tomorrow."

A little deflated he explained his visit to the field, which now seemed uneventful and not as terrifying as when he stood alone there. He quickly followed that with the two phone calls. It was a moment before Jones answered.

"Hm. Sounds suspiciously like the female lot we've been after, you know, the Mandy bunch. Now, is she the one that's done the supposed killing, or the one that's been seen off?"

"The ring leader?" Roger hesitated, "I must admit I'd never thought of her as running the show, but who knows?"

While he was musing, Jones cut in "And does the Bradley woman belong to that bunch?"

"It would make a lot fall into place if she is involved."

"And" Jones paused as he knew Williams wouldn't like the next bit, "has Bradley got anything to do with it?"

He got the reaction he expected. "I'm sure not. I've been keeping an eye on things, and he's round at Mrs. Stokes more than anything else, you know, where his daughter is staying."

"And he reported the wife missing?"

Roger jumped to his defense, "Well he would, if he was worried. What else could he do?"

"Alright, calm down." This was like lighting a touch paper. Perhaps the feeling the sergeant had experienced in the field had been stronger than he had wanted to accept.

"Look Roger, why not go round and speak to Bradley, I'll sort something out here and try and get to you by mid afternoon. O.K?"

Williams ventured, "And we'll go to the place, together, just in case?"
"Oh you can be sure we will." Jones replied but thought to himself "If only to get to the bottom of once and for all."

Vernon Treloar had been pushed slightly into the background with the morning's events. He was quite unaware of the attention he was receiving, but had he known he would have taken advantage of the temporary lack of interest. However, he had one purpose, spurred on by the lust placed in him by the evil one; he had to get to Lizzie. To possess her for ever, to make her his, and his alone.

It was just after lunchtime as he stood at Beth's front door, tapping gently. Expecting to see Robert, she opened it almost immediately and was surprised to see Vernon who never visited them.

"I'm sorry to bother you Mrs. Stokes, it was Lizzie I wanted a word with. It's about organizing something for the old folks for Christmas. She's good at that."
Having gathered her wits, Beth stood aside, "Oh please excuse me, I was expecting somebody else, do come in."

Following the morning's episode, Margaret had stayed in her room, and Lizzie was talking to her mother about Madge. They had discussed little else.
"Vernon, what are you doing here?" Lizzie came forward as he entered the room.

He accepted Beth's offer to sit down and explained that, with Christmas only two months away, they should start to sort out the festivities at the nursing home, and perhaps they could work on it together as he had some ideas for something a bit different.
"Oh that sounds wonderful Lizzie," Beth felt that this was just what her daughter needed. Something to get her teeth into, and helping the residents at the same time.

Lizzie was getting the strangest feeling. Almost drawn with an unseen attraction towards this man, a feeling that she had been close to him before. Her mind was searching its memory banks. The only thing she could resurrect was the time in the linen cupboard, but there seemed to be more, something here. But Vernon had never been here.

A slight noise made them all turn. There at the door was Margaret, her eyes fixed and glassy.

"What is it dear?" Beth was at her side in an instant.
"She hasn't been well" Lizzie explained, but as she spoke Vernon was already on his feet.

Margaret's mouth was open but no words came out. Instead she pointed straight ahead at the man now leaving. He had toyed with the idea of hypnotizing them all, but had a better plan.
"I'll see you again about this Lizzie," He patted her arm, "I can see your friend isn't well." He made his way to the door and left.

Beth and Lizzie helped Margaret to the settee, where she sat staring silently, her face white as though in shock.
"I'll ring her father" Beth hurried to the phone leaving her daughter to look after her friend.

She was amazed when he answered by saying the police were there. Her stomach churned. She explained about Margaret's reaction after being told of her mother's disappearance.
"It seems to have knocked her right back." she spoke almost in a whisper, then made Robert promise to ring her when he was free.

Within ten minutes he called back, saying he would rather speak to her face to face, but with Margaret's state he would explain on the phone, so that Beth could just relate as much as she felt necessary.

As he recounted what the sergeant had said, Beth felt weak. So was this where Madge had been going off to? It certainly explained the state in which she returned so many times of late. There was so much she wanted to ask, but with the girls in such close proximity had to hold back.

Robert realized this and said he would do the talking. It seemed that somebody had been killed during a black magic ritual, but whether it had anything to do with Madge they didn't know. It maybe just coincidence that it was today. Probably nothing at all.

He wanted to come to see Margaret but had promised to stay available at home, in case anything came to light.
"Keep in touch, at least we can talk by phone," Beth assured him Margaret would be alright, said good-bye and turned to the girls.

"Anything?" Lizzie looked up.
"Not yet. But I'm sure everything going to be fine." Her reassurance was shallow and not taken very much to heart.

Beth felt anger rise in her. Margaret had been right. Madge was to blame for everything, for the state the girl was now in, for the anguish she was causing. Oh how she must be enjoying it, laughing at them.

Unbeknown to any of them, Madge's ideal was far away, deeply repentant and begging for a chance to make amends for the sadness she had caused. But her pleading was in vain, for she was reminded that she was only sorry for herself, and had cared for nobody when she had the chance to show love. She was informed that she could not return until her next earth life, and until then she must exist in a holding area where she would have decades to regret the way she had let herself be ruled. From this she should learn many lessons before she would get another placing.

The ultimate powers knew that even after such a cleansing, it would make little difference to such a soul. As soon as she was re-positioned she would float to whatever force drew her. Such was her kind.

Zargot had returned to the holding zone, and upon witnessing the rows of lifeless hybrids, some scorched, some merely empty shells, his anger rose festering the hatred he felt towards the Eden spirals. There was only one ultimate being capable or willing enough to mastermind this, and that was Jenny. Once again he was in danger of her disrupting his reign of terror and he was ready for her.

His attention was drawn to the mass in the pit bottom. Realizing the concentrated evil contained in the welded hybrid remains, he wasted no time in harnessing the power for his own means, giving no consideration to the trapped ideals, knowing they would be no obstacle to him.

Leaving the useless part behind, he drove the combined entity earthwards, feeding it in bits through as many portals as possible, instructing it to spread illness, unhappiness, grief and destruction to the greatest extent possible.

Slightly satisfied, but with his anger still rising he thought "There you clever daughter of the Almighty One, see what you can do with that." So thinking he returned to his remaining forty eight functioning hybrids sitting just off the earth's atmosphere, waiting.

Jones arrived in Burford just before 4 o'clock.

"Sorry, couldn't get away before," he acknowledged Williams who closed the office door behind them.

"Glad you could make it. There isn't much daylight left." Roger wasn't looking forward to visiting the field again, but somehow he knew it was essential.

"Shall we talk on the way?" Jones wanted to get this sorted.

The sergeant grabbed a large torch from the shelf. "Just in case." he added.

They were soon on the Carterton road, and Roger quickly located the gateway, parked the car, and indicated for the chief to follow him. They crossed the road and entered the field, walking along the track leading to the trees.

Suddenly as if by unseen order, they both stopped dead. It was obvious to the younger man that his superior was experiencing the same as he, which afforded little consolation as the force now encircling them was much greater than that experienced when he was alone. But there was one important difference. This time, whatever it was, was not pushing him away, it was pulling them both further down the track. Their legs were moving involuntarily, carrying them towards the trees, until they found themselves running.

The chief stumbled on a clod of slightly raised earth and rolled to the ground, but still his momentum did not slow, for he rolled like a ball of tumbleweed, over and over. His companion was incapable of helping as he was being propelled at greater speed ahead. As he reached the trees, the force slowed him to a halt, and it was then he realized he was alone. Looking back he saw with horror the chief on his hands and knees being held back by the unseen power. It had separated them.

Instinct told the detective to rejoin his friend, but somehow he knew he would not be allowed. He looked down. At his feet were fresh tyre marks, and spiky indentations, obviously made by women's high heeled shoes. Bending down he noticed a few strands of blond hair which had been trodden into the soil and held there.

Again he looked towards the chief, who was now lying face down. He tried to retrace his steps to see if he was alright, but the force held him back so he ventured into the small wood firmly clutching his trusty torch. He followed the path made during the comings and goings of the coven, and was soon at the clearing.

It was gloomy, the trees forming a canopy over the space, and dusk was threatening to take over at any moment. Roger froze. There on a makeshift alter was what appeared to be the charred remains of a woman's body. So the anonymous caller had been right. Somebody had been killed, and by another woman, and it was in this area.

He knew he must look closer, so covering his nose and mouth with a handkerchief, he inched his way forward, and switched on the light. The sight that met him made him feel sick. Although the body was not completely burnt, the face was beyond recognition, the charred remnants of the clothes exposed the lower body, and the throat lay gaping where it had been sliced open.

Although it was hard to tell, Roger knew that there was a great possibility that this could be the mortal remains of Madge Bradley, and that she had been an active participant in some black magic ritual, resulting in her death. He looked around the immediate area. There were no signs of scorching on the undergrowth or trees, just in this spot. If somebody had wanted to destroy the evidence, they hadn't done a very good job. There was plenty here for forensic to get their teeth into, and it was therefore important to preserve the spot for their investigations.

As he realized he was no longer held by the unseen hand, his mind turned to the Chief Inspector. The half light had descended rapidly whilst he had been in the wood, and he had trouble in making out the form of the other man who appeared to be yards from where he had last seen him. It seemed to take ages to reach him, almost like a dream where you are trying to get somewhere, but however hard you run you are always in the same place. Eventually he fell at the side of him exhausted. Jones was still lying face down but well away from the track, and in the field. He did not move.

Roger shone his torch on him and tried to turn him over, recoiling with added horror as he did so. For the face of Det.Ch.Insp. Jones was badly burnt, although his clothing showed no signs of being in contact with any heat. At first he thought the man was dead, but realized that, although unconscious, he was still alive.

As the younger man rushed back to the car to radio in, his mind was churning. What power on earth could have caused this? But then as he slowed down an even worse fear hit him. It probably was not a power on earth, but something summoned by people wanting excitement, people like Madge Bradley who had now paid the price for such distractions.

Zena was furious. Being the Vexon that she was, she had to fuel her lust on a regular basis or somebody would feel the full power of her wrath. The recent death on her hands caused her no remorse. It was something she had exercised before when she had tired of some little plaything or other on earth or whatever planet the Vexons were occupying at the time.

During this inhabitation, she had moved around frequently, thus avoiding detection and escaping the silly little earth laws which would have curtailed her activities. One piece of homework was to always weigh up the opposition in the place of the moment. She was therefore well aware of Vedron's leanings, but didn't find the object of his intentions very interesting or she would have moved in and taken the prey.

He was not the smooth operator he would have people believe. Oh, he thought he was perfect, but he could only see what was before him, and therefore did not anticipate any threat or danger. As long as he was being satisfied, and could keep those in his power satisfied, he saw no need to complicate matters.

Zargot played these puppets for entertainment and pleasure, but found them valuable tools to carry out the physical evil emitting from his presence.

He now placed the insatiable longing for Hannah in Zena, and the reckless lust for Lizzie in Vedron. Ah Lizzie. He was looking at her now, holding her hand, sitting on the settee, and she was smiling at him. Tonight he would share her bed, so that he would not be alone. For now this would have to do until he could possess her using Vedron's body, but at this moment he was looking at her through the bodily eyes of Margaret.

CHAPTER 22

Jenny was well aware of the powerful wrath stirring in Zargot, and she knew it would not be long before she was locked in combat with the monster. She had played her cards well, gratified that she, with help, had managed to release so many trapped souls, but she would pay the price. Zargot would now be feeling humiliated again, and would strike back. But the question was always when?

Word had reached her that he was hovering around the Stokes household, but she was wary. Knowing this could be a trap to draw her, she held off. She also had kept Graham well away from the area in case Zargot should recognize his ideal as that of Hannah. Instead she had sentinels watching the remaining hybrids for the slightest move. It had entered her thought to pick them off where they were placed, but until she knew of their purpose, she decided to hold back. Furious at her for having destroyed the main force, Zargot could have re-programmed these in retaliation.

If she called in Schyning power, there was a possibility the electrical surge could be reversed and wipe them out. She dare not risk this. It was no game; the moves now were deadly serious. One slip and it could take aeons to restore the hold that the good forces had acquired.

Her attention could not slip for one tiny moment; for in that space of time, she knew her arch enemy would move in for the kill.

Mandy was nowhere to be found. In panic she had gathered all her belongings together and gone to stay with a friend in a neighbouring county. If Zena ever learned it was she who had made the anonymous call to the police, her fate could be worse than poor Madge's.

It was therefore Deana who now bore the brunt of the priestess's anger. Following the previous night's success the Vexon wanted more, and she wanted it now. She demanded that Hannah be brought to her so that her requirements be satisfied tonight.

"But I don't have a car, nor do you, we relied on Mandy's" the girl's voice trembled on the phone.
"Well fix it. Borrow one. Do what you have to, but remember this you little worm, to cross me is fatal, as well you know."

If only Deana had realized, she was so near to learning Zena's phobia. The leader had a fear of driving, and she could not travel in the front of a car, which was why she was always squashed into the back seat. This well kept secret could have been her downfall, but she was adamant that no-one would ever discover it.

"You mean you want me to find transport for tonight?" Deana answered in disbelief, "after all we -----"her voice trailed. She dare not take a stand against this female, so she quickly changed her tone, "I mean, does it have to be so soon?"

There was a long pause. "Perhaps I have not made myself quite clear." The words came out individually, loaded with venom. "When I say tonight, I mean tonight. Have you grasped it now?"

"Yes, yes, I'll sort it." she said but thought, "I don't know in God's name how."

"Good. We understand each other. Pick me up at seven thirty, usual place, then we will get the blond thing." The phone went dead leaving Deana looking at the handset for a moment before replacing it.

"I can't do it, I can't do it," she sobbed, "there's got to be another way." She had learned to drive and could get by at a push, but not owning a car she felt a little rusty. Besides, who would want to lend her one knowing her lack of experience? There had got to be another way.

She wasn't sure just how Hannah had arrived in Burford. Perhaps she had come by car, then everything would be alright. They could go in hers. Where was she staying? Quickly Deana thumbed through the telephone directory until she found the number of the hotel.

As the receptionist answered, it only then occurred to the caller that she didn't even know Hannah's surname.

"Could I speak to a lady staying there please? Her name is Hannah, she has blond hair, and she's been there a few days."

"I'm afraid we don't have anybody of that description madam. Are you sure you have the right hotel?"

Panic started to well up in Deana's stomach. "Of course I'm sure. We dropped her off there last night. I'm telling you she's staying there."

The calmness in the reply was from years of experience. "I'm terribly sorry madam, but I don't think we can help you." The call was ended.

Everything swam round before her as she sank to the floor, wondering how she could get out of this desperate situation. Mandy had done the best thing by getting away while she could, but why, oh why hadn't she given her the chance to go with her? She sat and viewed the hopeless situation. She couldn't get hold of a car. She didn't know where to find Hannah. But above all she was terrified of the ensuing wrath of Zena. There seemed no answer to it, or was there? Maybe she would have the last laugh over the evil woman, but unfortunately, she wouldn't be here to see it.

Although the Vexon didn't know it, it was in her favour that she was prevented from re-visiting her haunt that night, for it was now cordoned off by the scenes of crime officers who had taken charge of the wooded area and surrounding land.

The local farmer was none too pleased when he found out the two officers had entered his field without his permission, but he was taken on one side and had it explained to him that they hadn't wanted to arouse any suspicion in case there was nothing untoward. He was also told, quite firmly, that if he had been more diligent in who he had allowed to encroach, and for what purpose, he probably wouldn't now have a death on his property. The law didn't take kindly to landowners allowing such rituals.

Having had it put to him that way, he retracted his initial colourful remarks.

Detective Ch.Insp. Jones had been taken to the burns unit of the main hospital in Oxford, where his condition was described as stable. Whether he would ever work again following the inevitable skin grafting was highly unlikely, but one thing was certain, it had removed him from the scene, leaving Williams to fit the remaining pieces of the puzzle together.

Whilst more experienced officers were delving into the Carterton Road incident, he decided to get back on the tail of Treloar. It would be good therapy to have something to get his teeth into, or the recent experience could have left him somewhat shaken. Also, it would probably be his unenviable task to break the news to Robert Bradley if the body did prove to be that of his wife.

It was dark now, as the detective sat in his car watching Vernon's flat. There were no visible lights which suggested the occupant had already gone out.

"Missed him." Roger thought feeling a little deflated. He had hoped to follow at a distance, sure in his own mind that he would catch him red handed before long.

A movement made him start. In the shadows he could just make out a figure coming from the side entrance. No, it wasn't Treloar, different gait, much neater appearance, hair swept back exposing fine features. As the man set off, head high intent on his course, something made Roger's hand freeze on the ignition. Something he could only describe as a gut feeling nagged at him as his mind raced. Could this be how the rapist had gone undetected for so long? By changing his appearance. Of course. Hadn't he himself almost disregarded him?

Keeping his gazed fixed on the departing figure, Roger was mentally adding the vital points. Lizzie had said that she thought she knew the attacker but couldn't place him. Vernon Treloar worked alongside her, so she would know him. But if he was using hypnotism, she could be made to forget that fact, although the familiarity could nag at her subconscious.

His mind turned to Margaret. Treloar was a familiar face in the town, so she would be aware of him, if not knowing him. There again it could have been wiped from her mind.

Vernon was nearing the end of the street. Not wanting to draw any attention by starting the motor, Roger quietly got out and followed on foot keeping a safe distance. It didn't take long for him to realize his quarry was heading towards the Stokes home, not taking the well lit main street, but following the shadows in the back lanes.

Grateful that he had left the car, the detective pursued the man. He felt a little apprehension creep over him as the prospect of Robert Bradley possible visiting Mrs. Stokes could pose a problem. He quickly pushed that from his mind on two counts. Firstly, although he knew a body had been found, the husband didn't, and he could fend off any searching questions. Secondly, Bradley was supposed to be remaining at his own home awaiting any news.

Feeling a little safer in his own mind, he continued to track the man who was now speeding up his pace. Roger was amazed at the fitness of him, but realized that the job he did would keep him active.

Suddenly Treloar stopped. Roger dived into some nearby bushes pressing himself into the old foliage. He peered into the gloom. The fox was on the move again. He began to wonder if his presence was known and this fiend was merely leading him a merry dance.

But Vedron was not that clever. His one intention was the taking of Lizzie, tonight, by whatever means. He must achieve his goal, his total existence geared to success. Roger could have been walking directly behind him, he wouldn't have noticed.

Vedron was not going to bother with any fancy excuses. He would put all the women under his spell, and take Lizzie as before, except this time there would be two others to 'sleep' instead of one. He still wanted the object of his dreams to give herself willingly, but he would make her respond with his gentle orders, so it would be almost as good. At this time of night, it couldn't fail.

A gentle tap on the door made Beth start. Looking at her watch she said "It's almost ten o'clock. Who can it be at this hour?" But immediately guessed it must be Robert, although she wondered why he hadn't phoned if he had received news about Madge.

"Good evening Mrs. Stokes," the gentle lilt wafted into the room as the Vexon entered closing the door behind him. Still talking in his spell binding tones he eased Beth backwards until he could see she was going under. Easy so far.

"NO." The cry broke Beth from her trance and shook Vedron into swinging round to face the speaker. Margaret was on her feet, pointing accusingly at him.

Lizzie joined her. "What is it Margaret?"

"Him, it's him." Her finger still waved at Vedron who attempted to trance her where she stood, but she was to upset to succumb to his powers. "Don't you remember now? He did it. He raped you Lizzie."

Time appeared to slow almost to a halt. Lizzie looked from her friend to Vedron, recognition triggering her brain like lights being switched on.

Initially Beth was too stunned to move, but the protective mother instinct suddenly took charge. Without checking if the girls were sure, she flew at the Vexon like a wild cat. He was strong, but a mother of any species finds untold reserves when needed.

There was much pent up emotion in this household, and it had now found an outlet, an evil doer now turned into the victim. Within seconds all three females were upon him, releasing their hatred and revenge on this demon who had shattered their once peaceful lives.

Just what they would have done to him would never be known. At that moment the door was thrown open and the figure of Roger Williams framed the entrance. He quickly grasped the situation and managed to pull the women off, restraining Vernon on the floor.

He had followed the man, watched him enter the cottage, and listened for a moment at the door, witnessing the outburst and accusation which was all he needed for now. In no time his prisoner was taken away in a police van for questioning, but for now Roger needed to ease the information he required from these brave women.

Zargot viewed the scenes in the area. Zena's empire was temporarily disrupted with Mandy's departure followed by Deana. The priestess had disposed of the boring Madge, and her new prodigy Hannah had apparently disappeared from the face of the earth. If only she had known how correct she was. From experience, she recognized the signs and knew she too must depart from this town and start afresh in a new unsuspecting region. She imagined it would take a long time for the remains in the wood to be discovered, but if little whispers began to float around that something was going on in the area she had been using, it was best if she wasted no time in making herself scarce,

Zargot would follow her moves in case she came up with new pleasures for him, but for now he despised her amateurism, as he did that of the other Vexon. They merely played the game. He had watched Vedron's inefficiency in handling a situation by letting his lust take over solid reasoning and planning. But that is exactly what the evil one knew would happen, which is why they would always be manipulative tools in his hand.

He toyed with the idea that he might have had intervention from Eden, but knew that here he was dealing with a superior force. He still fumed at the destruction of his hybrids, but knew he still held the power to destroy the earth by his clever maneouverings. Yes, Jenny had enjoyed a clear run at the holding zone, but he knew she was being wary over the remaining holding craft still sitting off the earth. This time he knew he had her. Now she would have to bow to his ruling.

He viewed the Stokes household, but knew he would be better occupied elsewhere for the moment. The evil penetrating the earth from the massed J hybrid force was creating plenty of entertainment, and he had no wish to miss any of it.

After much deliberation, he had promoted Klee to the lower spiral on Zargon, knowing how much disruption this would cause among the other ultimates, but knowing it would also keep them occupied.

"Should prove quite amusing" he thought.

CHAPTER 23

The scenes of crime officers, when they were satisfied that all had been dealt with satisfactorily at site, supervised the removal of the corpse for further examination. The coroner's officer would have many questions, although not many would be answered verbally.

The activity had drawn attention to the field, and at first light on Sunday morning, a band of reporters were eagerly trying to be the first with any information but with little success.

Roger had agreed with the relevant officers, that in view of the possibility of public gossip, it would be kind to warn Bradley that a body had been found, especially as it was most likely to be his wife. An identification would be imminent, but he wanted to soften the blow a little by giving him time to take in the truth.

The meeting was far from pleasant, and although the detective tried to make it as tolerable as he could, he knew there was much more unpleasantness to follow, questions to which this man may or may not have the answers. Fortunately he seemed willing to talk, almost grateful to discuss the worry of the past few weeks with someone.

He related the change in his wife, her moods, her dress, adding his worry over the amount of pills she had started to take. Almost apologetically he confided that he no longer loved her, but quickly added that he never wanted her dead.

"If, it's her, who could have done it?" He looked pale, the reality of it beginning to show.

"That's what we intend to find out Mr. Bradley." Then very kindly "What about your daughter?"

"Margaret." Robert jumped up. "What can I tell her?"

"Well there is nothing positive yet. Do you want to wait until - well you know if the identification ----?"

"Yes. No. Oh look, it's driving me silly being here all alone. Would it be alright if I could be reached at Mrs. Stokes'?"

"I was going to suggest that." Roger smiled.
"I think I'd rather warn her, Margaret that is, prepare her, what do you think?"
"Good idea. Not only that, you will all be together." The sergeant hesitated. "Of course, my superiors will want a word, I'm only breaking the ice, you understand."
"Yes, yes, appreciate that. Your oppo not with you today then?"
This was something Roger didn't want to get into too deeply. "No, he's had a bit of an accident, be alright though I understand."
"Oh."
"So it will be somebody else that talks to you."
There was a silence. Roger decided not to push the identification matter just now, just in case it wasn't Madge, although he knew deep down it must be.

As he got up leave the detective asked if Robert was alright to drive, and being assured he was fine, the officer left, breathing a slight sigh of relief.
"That's the first bit over." he thought as he got into his car and headed back to the station.

As she received reports from her messengers, Jenny was concerned with the growing evil spreading over the earth at such a rapid rate. The good forces were fighting entities galloping in through ever open portals at an alarming rate, but in some cases the evil was so intense it was trampling over anything in its way. The ideals returned to Eden much the worse for wear unable to combat the increasing malice.

"I've got to stop this now" Jenny transferred the thought to the ultimates on the upper and lower spirals on Eden. Her father, the Almighty Power, had warned her again to combat the evil with love not hatred, reminding her not to become as destructive as the enemy. She had assured him she would exercise the necessary restraint, but he knew she would never rest in her fight to restore peace, a goal she could never really achieve.

Graham's previous scan of the moon had produced nothing informative, and although he had made many other quick visits, nothing appeared to be unusual. But something was still nagging at Jenny. There had to be a reason for the position of the hybrids and she was determined to find out what it was. Without further thought she switched to the moon's surface which always faces the earth. Slowly she let her being float over the surface, soaking up any disturbance of dust or change to the lunar landscape. Still nothing.

Feeling defeated she was about to switch back to Eden when she noticed a slight indentation, then another. Pulling back she could make out a line of perfect circles, about twenty in total. On closer examination she noticed five appeared deeper, and on moving along the row, each five seemed shallower than the last.

She mused for a moment. Had the same source caused all the circles, and was its power diminishing as it discharged its energy? In a flash the hybrids sprang into her thought. They could have been firing their lasers at the moon's surface, hence their holding position. But why the different depths?

She switched back to discuss her findings with the others. It was Marie who ventured "You are estimating the attacks to have all been made at the same time?"

"What are you thinking?" Jenny was grateful for this ideal's logic.

Matthew interrupted "And for what reason?"

Marie turned her attention towards the moon. "If they are holding in one position, they have to wait for the moon to orbit. They are not travelling with it."

Jenny jumped. "You mean each time it comes round they fire at it?"

Graham had been calculating all this and queried "So each time the power is a little less causing less depth of disturbance?"

"No." Jenny's ripple of thought hit the others with such an impact; they all knew she must have worked out the reason for such an apparently innocent action. All waited for her next communication.

"The attacks were not made on reduced power. The intensity was the same, but the target had moved, each time it was further away."

Silence. The enormity of Jenny's supposition was horrendous. After letting the first thought sink in, she continued. "We know the moon is moving slowly away from the earth, but in its present position it is holding the earth on the axis and stabilizing it. Likewise we on Eden, sitting just behind the moon but travelling with it, are also stabilized."

Graham asked. "So if it is moving, or being moved away from the earth, and towards us, our spiritual area is in the utmost danger of being thrown off line?"
Matthew agreed. "It's all being done gently isn't it? So that we won't notice."
Marie joined his wave "Until it's too late?"

Jenny affirmed all this with "So apart from earth devastation, it's probably Eden he's out to destroy. I wonder if this was pre-planned, or retaliation for the destruction of the hybrids." Although she didn't want to admit it, her father's words flicked through her being like a scolded child receiving a punishment.
"It would be my fault." She kept the feeling to herself, but the weight of it was beginning to tell.

It didn't take the police long to get the evidence they needed to prove Vernon Treloar was the attacker they had been seeking. His sample of semen matched the stains found at both of Lizzie's rapes, but he was not forthcoming about the attack on Margaret.

Roger Williams stood with a senior detective at the door of the Stokes' home, knowing he had good and bad news. Beth opened the door and immediately beckoned the officers to enter. Robert was there as agreed, but looking very drawn, and the two girls sat huddled in their usual place. Although it was Monday, none of them felt like going to work in view of the recent happenings. Little was said as the two men sat down, the assembled party guessing almost what was coming. The senior man, being new to the set up, verified the identity of the Bradley family, then calmly explained that the body found appeared to be that of Mrs. Bradley. There was a shudder through the room. Lizzie hugged Margaret, who was sobbing to herself, not hysterically, but from sadness now. Beth comforted Robert then went to the two girls to see if they were alright.

Roger took this opportunity to speak to the father. They would take him to identify the remains, but warned that it wasn't pleasant, and would explain on the way. Then in a louder voice "The left hand was in pretty good shape, and there are two rings which you may recognize." He didn't go into detail that it had been estimated they could not have been placed there after death, for when a ring has been worn for several years, it leaves a groove in the finger. Such marks showed that both rings belonged to the wearer.

"Do you want me to come with you?" Beth offered but Robert shook his head. "No, I'll see to it." He got his coat and turned to Roger, "It won't take long will it?"
"Not the actual business, but we do have to go to Oxford."

As they prepared to leave, Williams turned to Beth and said "Perhaps not the best time to tell you, but the Treloar chap has confessed." Then to Robert, "One weight off your mind anyway."

Within seconds the men had departed, leaving Beth and the girls to their grief.

Klee looked in on this unhappy little scene with pleasure. Might be amusing to take over one of these sad people. She looked at Margaret. A bit pathetic although a good candidate for a little mischief and in her present state she would be wide open for possession.

Lizzie? A bit simple but manipulative. Not impressed she turned her attention to Beth. Ah, a challenge. If she could corrupt this 'holier than thou', person, it could only be to her credibility in her new role, and provide a little sadistic entertainment on the way. Wouldn't Zargot be pleased?

Had she only known that Zargot's next target was Robert Stokes, she may have played further afield. Knowing the man to have been cleared of the rapes on his daughter and her friend, it would leave the evil one an open door to move in and take over a seemingly good man. If he didn't, part of the J hybrid malice would do it for him, and that could never be allowed.

Due to the severity of the findings in the wood, extra special officers had been called in to carry out extensive investigations. Although they didn't actually voice it, they thought the local CID man could easily overlook things which were familiar to him, things that they would question at every move.

As soon as they could, they would go over the Bradley house with a tooth comb, taking away whatever they considered evidence.

For now they were concerned with tracing whoever was party to the murder, for that's what it was now officially classed as. They had a few leads. Apart from the detective's shoe prints at the spot where the car had been parked, they noticed imprints of several different footwear, including the boots worn by Hannah. Graham had diligently removed some blond strands from his wig while pretending to toy with the locks. He hoped he had trodden them well into the ground, being unable to check for himself. Sure enough they had been found and taken away along with other minute bits and pieces.

One important item missing was the object used to slit the victim's throat. If only they could find that. Even microscopic traces of blood would prove invaluable.

From information supplied by Roger's reports, they decided to track down this Mandy person, expecting her to be well involved, but they soon learned from her landlady that she had "upped and gone off."

"She didn't leave an address at all?" The officer was not one to be fobbed off easily.

"Like I said, nothing. Here one minute gone the next. Mind you, she was always coming in late." The woman grabbed the chance to relay any gossip.

"Do you know where she went, when she was out late?" A gentle prod should help thought the detective.

"Well, "the woman looked up and down the street, and before she could continue, the officer had asked if they could continue the conversation away from prying eyes. His kindly approach soon led her to inviting him to see the girl's room.

"I haven't done much with it yet, just stripped the bed. Sorry it's such a mess."

Leading the woman to the door he whispered "I'd be most grateful for a look through anything she may have left. Thank you so much."

Before she realized she was outside the closed door, wondering what was going on. She certainly would have a tale to tell her cronies when she saw them.

The cupboards and drawers were empty and it was obviously Mandy had left in a rush as she hadn't closed anything properly. Odd bits of useless stuff lay on the floor. An empty tights packet, and old comb, sweet wrappers, but nothing of significance. The man's attention was then drawn to an item which often yields the most information, the waste basket. As he carefully sifted through the discarded bits he stopped at one piece of crumpled writing paper. Smoothing it out on his leg he read the beginning of a note.

Dear Deana,
Sorry to run out on you like this, but she'll have us next. Last night was the end, I can't take any more. Do the same, get out while you can or Zena will—

the writing trailed off.

Questions jumped into this trained officer's mind.
Why wasn't the note sent? Was this only a scrapped one, with the final copy already on its way to Deana? Or did Mandy leave in too much of a hurry to send or deliver it? That sounded more likely. This Zena sounded a force to be reckoned with. But now they had two more names to chase up, together with handwriting and fingerprints on one little scrap which could so easily have been destroyed.

Before he left, the detective got a brief description of Mandy's car. Although the woman didn't know one make from the other, being the busy body that she was, she noticed other important details.
"It was a brightish blue, not very special, but it had a doll dangling in the front window."
As a long shot the policeman asked "I don't suppose you have any idea as to the number?"
"Well, it's funny you should ask that, because you see the letters were my late husband's initials." She seemed satisfied at the fact not seeing the reason to continue.
"And they were?" Time for another gentle prod.
"Oh, silly me. HAT. Harry Alfred Thomas. But don't ask me what the numbers were. I'm no good on remembering numbers."
"Well, you've been very helpful Mrs. Thomas. Maybe I can come back if there's anything else you can think of." Leaving his phone number he returned to his car satisfied at having drawn another fragment out of the bag.

CHAPTER 24

The next few days were by no means easy. Robert spent a lot of time at Beth's, none of them having any wish to visit his home more than was necessary. The place had been turned upside down and many of Madge's belongings taken away for examination. The funeral was on hold whilst more enquiries were made and every new fact unearthed seemed to produce more sadness.

At the same time, Lizzie and her friend were being questioned about Vernon Treloar. This time even Beth's pleading could not shield Margaret from the onslaught although the women officers did their best to be understanding with her.

Lizzie was almost feeling sorry for her attacker saying he had always been kind to her. This made the police wonder again if she had actually given in to him at any stage but on being questioned she didn't think she could have as she wanted to 'save herself' as she put it.

Margaret stood up to the ordeal fairly well, but had no idea who Treloar's friends could have been when it was suggested to her that it could have been a gang that attacked them on the first night. Nothing triggered in her mind, so it was presumed they were unknown to her.

But there was one person who could divulge their identity, and that was the man himself. He would be made to talk, by whatever means necessary.

Beth stood watching as the girls finished with the questioning. For the first time in her life, she eyed Margaret with such disgust, almost as if it had been Madge she was looking at. Shaking the feeling from her, she moved to place a comforting arm around them both

Robert too was eyeing his daughter, not with the fatherly protection he had cherished since she had been born, but with the lustful look of one who must have her. He too pushed away such thoughts, wondering if this was some evil spirit Madge had aroused during her escapades.

Klee and Zargot faced each other. Both unable to sustain the desired effect in their chosen victims, they blamed each other for their simultaneous possession, but it was Zargot who expelled his new recruit from the scene, warning her never to meddle in what was his. She did not wait to be ordered again, but returned to Zargon angry, much to the delight of both spirals.

The one thing that the evil entities had not taken into account, was the intense love shared between the two parents and their daughters. When together, they created a protective combined aura, and although it had been momentarily penetrated, the forces had been evicted by the sheer goodness of the hosts.

The Almighty One looked down from his throne, satisfied with the intervention from the topmost ideal of the upper spiral. Again his teaching had proved the victor.

"Love rules, and must always conquer hate," was his message down the line, knowing it would not escape Jenny's attention.

It was becoming an urgent fact as the weeks passed, that some arrangement had to be made regarding living requirements. Robert had stayed at Beth's, sleeping on the settee, but it was obvious that things could not remain like that.

They had all drawn strength from each other during the arduous period which covered the eventual funeral, enquiries to trace Mandy, Deana and Zena, all of which had come to nothing. The police had frequently asked Robert's help every time a new scrap of a lead was discovered, but nothing now triggered anything of use.

Vernon Treloar was to be brought to trial. Even in view of the damming evidence he was pleading innocent, which meant the girls would be brought as witnesses. Roger Williams had a feeling that once again this creature would escape the net of the law. With good representation, knowing both girls had been hypnotized and could therefore not give a positive identification, he could get off. But the detective's hopes were raised when he remembered that now there were the stains against the accused. Surely this time. But he had learnt never to cheer until the sentence was passed.

Christmas had come and gone, and although everyone tried to make the most of it, none had much heart for festivities.

Robert had made one of his few visits to his house, just to check that everything was in order. There had been a few frosts of late, and he was worried about water pipes with the place empty. He gladly returned to the welcoming fireside at Beth's cottage. As usual all four sat round the glow.

"I don't want to say this," he started" but something's got to be done about No.8." as he referred to the home he had shared with Madge.

"Oh Dad," Margaret started, but Beth intervened.

"Better now dear, it's getting worse as time goes on."

"The thing is," Robert hesitated "well, Beth and I have been talking and---" he wasn't allowed to finish, for Lizzie started bouncing with excitement.

"You're going to get married aren't you? You are. Say you are."

Beth couldn't hide the smile. "Slow down, it's not that simple."

Both girls now were talking over each other, "Why not? We are happy together. You can't spilt us up."

Robert held up his hand. "Think of what it will look like." There was a silence.

Lizzie looked dazed; she could only see the happiness that could be in store for them all.

Beth took over. "Lizzie, Margaret. Yes we love each other and we love both of you."

"So why not ------?"Lizzie tried again but Beth continued. "Just think of what has happened, not that I need remind you. But what might people, like the police, think if we hurried things too much."

"Oh no." Margaret was a little quicker on the uptake. "They might say you had --- Oh Dad, no!"

Beth had foreseen this and quickly took charge again. "We know dear, but there are some nasty people out there, as we are now well aware. Let's not spoil our happiness by playing into their hands eh?"

The two girls looked at each other, Lizzie now understanding, both smiled and nodded, then turned to their parents and agreed for the delay, but only if they could be bridesmaids when the day came. Beth actually threw back her head and laughed, the first time for weeks.

"What do you make of this pair Bob?"
For the first time he embraced her in front of anyone. "I think that we are so lucky, and I wouldn't change them for the world."

Immediately they were all hugging, a few little tears of relief and joy appearing on each cheek.

Zargot had laid many plans, but it was the earthly ones which were occupying his present attention. Having sent Klee back for a cooling off period, he could concentrate on crushing the Eden power once and for all. Then he would rule alone. After conquering the earth he could move on, but every time he had come anywhere near to this in the past, she, Jenny, had intervened. But not any more. This time he had the J6 mass, whose evil was festering and growing at a pace even he had never experienced. As long as he stayed in charge, nothing could go wrong. Self gratified, he proceeded to set his trap.

Jenny felt somewhat reprimanded. She knew her father would always insist that love could conquer all, and she was well aware of the power of it, but she was also equally aware of the evil power which was now sniffing her out, goading her to make the first move. The evil one would be aware she had discovered the moon attacks, and know that she would not let her attention slip from that part while the hybrid craft were still in position. So what if this should all be a red herring, just something to keep her occupied while he laid his plans elsewhere, and then strike while her back was turned? The game was becoming like a huge chess board, each player waiting for the other to move in turn.

It was settled. There wasn't enough room at the cottage for four grown people to live comfortably on a permanent basis, and neither Robert nor Margaret relished the idea of going back to No.8 to live. The Stokes ladies too would never have felt comfortable in such surroundings.

It was quite a relief for Robert and Beth to at last be able to show their feelings for each other, but in view of recent discussions, it was agreed to keep it between the four of them for now.

The obvious arrangement would be to eventually sell No.8 and the cottage, and buy another house maybe just outside of Burford where they could all make a fresh start. In the meantime there was much to be done. Madge's belongings would have to be disposed of, for nobody wanted anything that reminded them of the recent trauma. Robert assured Beth that he would keep nothing of their early mementos. He needed to put it all behind him and start life with the woman he had always loved, something in his wildest dreams he never imagined could have come true.

It was still January, and although the sun fought bravely to warm the air, the chill couldn't be ignored. Beth stood at Robert's side as he unlocked the front door of his house. He didn't call it a home anymore.

"Oo, needs airing." was her first reaction, "it's very cold, let's get some heat on."

They had decided to tackle the first onslaught alone, and offer Margaret any of her mother's jewellery etc. that she might like to keep.

Robert switched on a gas fire in the lounge. "This'll do for now, it'll take the central heating a long time for us to feel the benefit."

"Where do you want to start?" Beth felt uneasy being here and wanted to get the job done as quickly as possible.

"The worst first." Robert took her hand to lead her upstairs. "I was thinking of the bedroom," he noticed her hesitation, "I'll do it alone if you'd rather."

"No, it's not that." She shivered. Thinking she was still cold he put his arm around her, drawing her to him.

Her whisper just reached his ear. "I don't like it. Can't you feel it, or is it just me being silly?"

His laugh floated over her hair. "It's you. Look this isn't easy, I shouldn't have asked you."

"You didn't, I offered remember." Pulling away and giving herself a shake she laugh back "It's gone now, whatever it was. Let's get on with it."

"You've been cooped up in that cottage too long my girl, time I got you out of it." He turned and ran up the stairs, Beth on his heels chasing him, giggling like a couple of school children.

The nursing home had very understanding with Lizzie, allowing her to take what time she needed to get herself straight, but glad to have her back. Some of the residents had got all the usual winter ailments and her help was invaluable. Shock waves had hit the establishment when they learned of the goings on of their handyman, apart from which they would miss his work which had been always been satisfactory. Matron was certain that any replacement would be well vetted. Lizzie soon slipped back into her role, where she felt needed, and appeared to be none the worse for any of her recent experiences.

Margaret had left her previous employer, not knowing how long it would take for her to get back on even ground again. She couldn't face meeting people, so many of the few vacancies were unsuitable for her in her present state.

Beth didn't push her, but was also aware that the longer she hid away in the cottage, the more difficult it would be for her to start again. It was Lizzie who solved the problem. She came bouncing in one evening announcing that she was starving, as usual, and that the lady who popped in to help with the teas had had to rush off because her husband was ill, and they could have done with somebody to wash up.

Margaret popped her head out of the kitchen. "I'd have done that, if you were stuck." The other two ladies tried not to show their delight. Lizzie said slowly "She only comes in for an hour or so, but if she's not there, we have to pull it in, and it's just at a busy time."

The main topic of conversation over the meal was confined to this. Robert had arrived in the middle of the chatter, and he too had to hide his relief that this could be the first glimmer of light in his daughter's step back to normality.

It was agreed that Lizzie would have a word with matron the following day, and if Margaret could help, she was readily available.
"What are you doing tonight Mum?" Lizzie asked as she helped clear away the plates.
"We were going to No 8. The main sorting's been done but there are a lot of papers, and old bills that need throwing away. Margaret's dad thought this was a good time as any for a complete clear out, after all he doesn't want to bung up our new home with old stuff that's irrelevant."
"We could come." Lizzie sounded eager.
Beth hesitated and looked from her to Margaret and then to Robert.

It was Margaret who spoke. "I don't mind. I could clear my old room if you like. Liz could help, couldn't you Liz?"
Robert smiled. "This prospect of the possibility of a little job at the nursing home seems to have done wonders. Of course you can come."
"That's settled then." Beth had the feeling for the first time that things might just be moving for the better. They hurriedly cleared the table, washed up and got ready for the evening's task.

The latest wave of terror created by the J's was concentrated in North America. Identical reports were filling the news of so-called religious cults indulging in mass suicides, many of the victims being teenagers and small children, their lives cut short in the most horrible way.

Enquiries produced little accurate evidence as most deaths had been covered by an intense fire, hopefully destroying all clues. But thanks to modern science, the forensic teams sifted tirelessly through the gruesome remains and came up with some very startling facts.

It appeared that in certain areas the victims were shot or stabbed first, maybe during some sort of ritual, then the place set alight by one remaining disciple before ending their own life.

In other cases it was suspected the people were poisoned first, but there again it would be easy to administer anything if the followers thought they were taking part in some black communion.

Marie's helpers were taxed to the limit, overseeing the ones in transition and although Jenny was drawn to become involved, she was third in line in the upper spiral, taking into account the Almighty One was always in permanent position at the very top, and it was therefore not her turn to take an active part. She was still overseeing the hybrid craft positions and Zargots whereabouts, but from her home station, relying on the continual reports being fed to her by her trusty workers. If the earth activity was Zargot's enticement to draw her down, he would be disappointed. But she needed positive reassurance that this was his doing, and not just the evil J's spreading their own destruction.

The ultimate at the second place of the spiral was dispatched to cover the American slaughter, and Jenny moved up so that she was just where she needed to be. She hoped nothing else would occur to occupy her in the meantime while she was waiting and watching.

CHAPTER 25

The party of four entered No.8. in quite high spirits. They were all treating this job as something to get out of the way to pave the path to their future happiness.

Without any cue from either parent, the two girls galloped upstairs to clear Margaret's room of any remaining knick knacks. Robert smiled lovingly at Beth and they slowly followed, wrapped in their own affection, but with each step they felt something pushing them back. It took all Robert's strength to hold the two of them against the banister to prevent them being hurled backwards. What happened next sent a chill through them both, they would never forget.

A strangled scream came from Margaret, now standing rigid near the bedroom previously used by Madge. Lizzie was clutching her in absolute terror, her mouth wide, searching for a cry that never came.

With every ounce of effort, the two parents willed themselves upwards. "Push, fight it." Robert felt he had to shout as if in a gale, and Beth responded with all her might. Neither knew just what they were fighting, but it didn't matter, they had to get to the girls. As they reached the landing, exhausted they froze. They could barely see Lizzie or Margaret for the mist which enveloped them, swirling, choking. In horror they could only watch as the mist solidified into a hideous form resembling the wide eyed hybrids but far more terrifying. It waved around, its' many spindly limbs stretching out to grab anything in its path. Above all it emitted the most sickening stench, its evil spreading like molten lava to entrap all in its way.

Beth was crying with fright. All she could see was the disappearing shape of Lizzie being melted, swallowed, and devoured by this vile entity.

The heinous thing had tried to separate the four and had almost succeeded in doing so. It was again, only the intense love they shared which pulled them together, but they alone could not fight the concentrated evil now taking possession. It moved nearer to the parents.

Something triggered simultaneously in each of their minds. "Love. Think only of the love." They received a command as Matthew and Graham entered their bodily forms and merged with their ideals. They pushed the fear back and concentrated all their combined power, directing intense love and pure vibrations at the fiend. When Beth wavered slightly, Matthew took over, injecting more power on her behalf.

They would never have been able to estimate how long it took, for the next moments seemed like hours, but slowly the thing retreated, shrinking as it did. Marie was on hand, and at the precise moment was able to extract the fragmented ideal struggling to escape. She pulled it free, handing it to an experienced helper, knowing the care that would be needed to see it finally over.

As it left the piece of J mass, the evil contracted and was pounced upon by Graham as he left Robert's body. Matthew quickly followed and they were joined by five other ideals that formed an invisible circle around the being and exorcized it in much the same way as closing a portal. As the evil left the earth limits, it was dispatched by other forces to a place where it would be destroyed, never again to corrupt any living form. It was sent to join Johhahn in the same black hole.

Jenny had been monitoring the activity, glad now that she had sent her reliable sources to cope with it. This fragment of evil had entered through the portal in the wood and lay dormant and unnoticed waiting for the right moment to strike, and it had found it. Zargot had not been the instigator of this latest attack, and Jenny was relieved she had still held back. It would have been so easy to have been drawn into this, but the two had handled it perfectly.

She was not surprised to receive a reminder from above that it had been the force of concentrated love that had triumphed again. "Yes Father." she tried to keep the sarcasm from the thought but knew it would not go unnoticed.

Margaret and Lizzie lay in a crumpled heap pressed against the bedroom door. The air was clear with no sign of mist or image of anything untoward. The presence had left the place, leaving the atmosphere drained but clean.

Beth was first to rush to the girls, who still did not move, and fearing for their safety she became hysterical, shaking them and shouting for them to respond. Robert was with her as soon as he gathered his wits.
"Tell me they aren't dead Robert." The tears streamed down her face.
"No, look they are coming round." Each parent coaxed their daughter back to consciousness, kissing and hugging them as they gained their bearings.
Terror spread over Margaret's face. "What happened Dad?"
"Sh, sh now." He stroked her head. "There was something, but it's gone now. Everything's alright."
"Mum." Lizzie looked up weakly but feeling the strength return.
Beth was rocking her in her arms as if she was still the baby she had nursed.
"It's alright." was all she could say.
Robert took charge, his fright now turned to anger. "I bet she had something to do with this."
"Who?" Beth felt a little more secure now.
"Let's be honest," he looked at both girls, " they said Madge had possibly, no definitely been dabbling in the occult. Well we don't know to what extent, but mark my words, she's at the bottom of this."
"Oh Robert," Beth shook her head in disbelief, "don't say that."
"Well, what other explanation is there? It's only here. Alright it's gone now."
"Will it come back Dad?" Margaret was still trembling.
"We're not going to find out. I'm sure it's gone for now, but we're not waiting around. Come on get anything you want to take and that's it. We're not coming back."

They all quickly grabbed as much as they could, bundled it into the boot of the car and were gone. The only time Robert would return would be to sell the place, and then he would leave it in the hands of the estate agents if possible.

As they all settled over a much needed cup of tea at the cottage, it was Lizzie who made the strange statement.
"I don't know how to say it."
"Say what dear?" Beth was wondering what was coming now.

"Well, somebody was with us, helping us. Did you feel it Margaret?"
Her friend put her cup down. "Yes, it was all lovely and warm and protective, and it was fighting the cloud, but I felt ever so safe."
"Yes so did I, then we seemed to go to sleep, and when we woke up it was gone."

Beth and Robert exchanged glances. "What sort of somebody?" The mother was curious in view of her own experience.
The girls looked at each other and shrugged, then Lizzie said "Somebody nice and loving, just like you really Mum, only it couldn't have been you could it?"
"We'll probably never know," Robert finished his tea and indicated for Beth to pour him another cupful, "but the main thing is, we're all here, we're alright, and if a guardian angel was protecting us, let's hope it stays."
"That's a lovely way of putting it Bob," Beth inclined her head, little knowing that it wasn't the first time Jenny's forces had been referred to as angels.

"They've turned". The message that was received on the upper Eden spiral sent a wave of interest fluttering through the ultimates.
"All of them?" Jenny wanted to know.
"Not exactly." The messenger was a little hesitant.
"Explain."
"They appear to be doing it in rotation, along the line, a few at a time. But when the complete line is turned, they start all over again."
Jenny mused. "What's he playing at?"
"Also, there are forty five now."
This brought Jenny's attention to a jolt. "And where are the other three?"
The messenger paused again. "We think one of Zargot's devils has taken them, or borrowed them, we can't trace them at the moment."
Jenny could have been angry but she curbed her instinct. "Didn't any of you notice? You were supposed to have a continual watch between you."
"Yes. But we think it was during the turn arounds. They sort of do a little circuit, and as one batch are repositioning into the line the next are moving as well and - it must have been then."
"They fooled you." Jenny could not resist the cutting thought.

"Not the craft. But the others didn't help." The servant was gently putting the case forward.
"What others?"
"The three ultimates from Zargon. There was that new one, Klee and two others, they seemed to be fighting over control of some of the craft, and we were confused as to whether Klee took over the three missing ones or if they took one each, there was a lot of arguing, it got quite nasty."

"So" Jenny was quite pleased now. "The Master isn't getting it all his own way. This new creature may be as disruptive as the last." Then before dismissing her worker, she enquired "What about the moon?"
"They don't seem to have aimed at it again."

Left alone Jenny summed up the events. She wasn't absolutely certain that the moon activity was a decoy. There had been too much energy used, plus the fact the moon had been moved slightly. But this could have been a sample of Zargot's power. A threat for later. A warning.

Roger Williams flicked through the latest reports of renewed cult activity. He felt sure that many such happenings were only as a result of the media interest, and many covens if they were not that serious, would fizzle out after a short while.

He shuddered as he remembered the horrible ending endured by Madge Bradley and his mind turn to the others of the sect. From the information passed on to him by the seconded officers, Zena was in charge, and this Mandy woman and Deana whoever she was seemed to be under her control. The three had apparently vanished from the face of the earth. A smile cross his lips as he wondered how appropriate that idea might be.

The sharp ringing of the telephone interrupted his concentration. "Now what?" he thought. The past months had left him feeling in need of a holiday, and he was not in the mood for any in depth discussion at the moment.
The caller quickly identified himself as the detective who had visited Mandy's lodgings.
"Just thought you'd like to know, the blue car," he gave the registration number including the HAT "has been sold to a dealer down in

Cirencester. The woman must have moved fast to get rid of it before we could circulate it."
"So that leaves us where exactly?" Roger stifled a yawn.
"The Mandy woman could be somewhere in that area, although the description seems altered. As to the leader of the pack, if she is used to quick departures, she could have set up her stall anywhere in the country, under a new identity and most likely she will have changed her appearance as well."

Roger wondered why the man had called. He didn't seem to have anything earth shattering to impart, so perhaps he just wanted to prove he had been doing something before admitting the trail had run cold.

Trying to sound a little enthusiastic he said "So that just leaves the other one, Deana somebody."
"Ah. Now that's more interesting."
"Oh?" Roger wondered what was coming.
The detective was savouring this titbit, almost dangling it. "It seems the two underlings of this Zena character were running scared. Remember I told you about the part note I found?"
"How could I forget?" Roger thought but replied "Yes. Go on."
"We've had another one, but handed to us."
"You have, but why, and who gave it to you?"
"It seems this Deana wasn't going to hang around to take the flack when she knew her friend was off. So she wrote to her mother saying she had got in with the wrong crowd and needed to get away for a while."
"Was she more specific?" Roger still felt this was all a bit to thin to hang anything on.
"Not to her mother. But she enclosed a note which she asked her ma to give to us, but only after she had enough time to get well away."

Roger was interested now, and wished the detective had come to the point sooner. "And the contents?"
"We didn't open it in front of the mother you understand, good job too. The letter was addressed simply to 'The Police'. It outlined in detail the events leading up to Mrs. Bradley's murder. Yes, she witnessed it."
"Did she describe the state of Madge Bradley? I mean are you sure?"

"Oh, no doubt about it. Seems she was in a drugged sort of state, but the torture preyed on her mind, and she felt she would be next if she hung around. Course, she didn't know the Zena woman had gone too."
"Can you tell me how she described it?"
"Oh it's all there, the candle up the vagina, the throat slit from ear to ear. Frightened her, make no mistake."
Roger had waited patiently but now needed to know a most important fact. "Did she describe the torching?"
There was a pause and he knew he had something the other man may have overlooked in his so called thoroughness.
"No. Don't think that was there. Shouldn't worry though, it means we know it was murder, from one who was there. All we've got to do is find her, she's a witness."
Roger took a breath. "That's very good, a very adequate description except...." Now it was his turn to dangle his fellow officer.
"Um, in what way?"
"Whoever, or whatever scorched the body and the clothing, did so after the women left, or Deana would have certainly mentioned it."

As he ended the call, Roger replaced the receiver slowly, the facts chasing around his brain. He must have come so close to nailing these females. If only he had gone out onto the Carterton Road on the Friday night and not left it until the Saturday. But he had been intent on catching Treloar, which he had now achieved, but the nagging that the man would escape his just desserts again kept prodding him like toothache.

He weighed up the two cases. Would it have been better, with hindsight, to have maybe prevented Madge's death by intervention, than catch this sex fiend? Whichever way he looked at it, the Bradley's were involved in some way, even by being victims. Robert was a nice chap but what difference did that make. From Roger's experience in the force, the innocent ones were often the losers.

As he left the station, he could not shake the feeling of failure from his shoulders, which was exactly the feeling Zargot had planted.

CHAPTER 26

The farmland murder would be recorded for future reference in many minds, but as with most things, local people's personal events soon pushed it into the background, and within weeks it was yesterdays' news.

A little lad had since slipped into the river and nearly drowned, so the last thing on his parents' mind was some silly people playing at being witches. One of the antique shops on the High Street had been broken into, and with the usual minor road traffic accidents to cope with, the police were kept fairly busy.

Spring was on the way, and for anyone taking a nature ramble in this part of the country, there was always plenty to see.

Margaret had slipped comfortably into her little job at the nursing home, and feeling secure in her surroundings soon proved she could be quite an asset. Matron realized that the washing up task was merely a rehabilitation period, and, provided the girl was not rocked by any more metal stress, she could make something of herself.

There was the usual stack of paperwork awaiting the matron's attention, and as she thumbed through the top sheets she stopped. Perhaps Margaret could be of help in the small office, but the experienced woman was eager not to put Lizzie down, although knowing she was suited to the jobs she had been given, and probably little else.

"I'll start her off with some simple filing and typing notices," matron decided but making a note to find Lizzie a little something important at the same time.

Although the time was dragging on, Jenny knew she dare not slip in her concentration, for that was when the evil power would surely choose to strike. She was aware that he had moved his main activities away from England, now wanting bigger areas to corrupt in one go, and he was succeeding. The little country happenings had been a good rehearsal to introduce his hybrids, but when he remembered how few were left, his anger rose.

However, he had been given a bonus. The sadistic J's had more than compensated for the loss in number of the basic forms. The sad ideal that had been released during the No.8. episode had not affected the ghoulish remains. In normal circumstances, when a spirit or ideal leaves a body in transition, the vehicle used is said to be dead. But the entities created were now self motivated and the five remaining trapped souls were going through a living hell until they could be extracted.

Also, the evil did not necessarily need physical matter to transport itself. It learned it could perform to greater terror by producing images and mental imbalance than by being attached to a mass. Zargot was aware of this development and tried to stay master of this evolution of evil, but the entities appeared to be reproducing at an alarming rate.

They took it upon themselves to discard anything containing their passengers, the five remaining ideals, thus letting the poor things finally take the path to peace. Marie rejoiced at this, but Jenny knew this could only mean something big was brewing.

Again the questions churned. Was it Zargot's doing, or was he now being used as a pawn? Who was she fighting? Who was now in charge? This could well account for the lull. If the evil master was occupied in staying in control of his own court, she could have been put aside for the time being. It occurred to her that this could be the time to catch him at his weakest and lead the attack, but her father's teaching reminded her that this was not to be.

"But it doesn't stop me watching" she decided as she dispatched her sentinels over the earth to scan the activities, and report back.

Her attention turned to the hybrids, still waiting in position. Klee had enjoyed her little bit of fun, playing with the three craft and had now returned them to their original places. It proved how easy it had been. Should she have need of the things, she knew she could take as many as required and put them back if she wanted.

Jenny was aware of this tactic and knew she must give the being enough attention to be aware of her movements, but not be drawn away from the matter in hand, so she delegated Matthew to monitor the little upstart.

Robert had taken temporary lodgings for the time being. By mutual agreement he could no longer stay at the cottage, could under no circumstances return to No.8. and it was too soon to marry Beth for the sake of decency. Margaret would stay where she was for now, as the two girls had been through so much, and things were taking an upward trend with them working together, it seemed a pity to split them. The two monkeys delighted in teasing Beth about her love, but she was only too happy to soak up the banter now things could only get better. The hope of a sublime future was in store, and not before time, and she was going to see that nothing would mar their happiness.

The tornadoes which were ripping through the townships in the eastern states of America were leaving trails of utter destruction. A whole area of houses could be flattened, trees stripped leaving an air of complete silence and devastation as the survivors sifted broken hearted through piles of rubble which had once been homes.

Even the hardest of people could not have believed the sheer joy achieved by the J's as they wallowed in the pain they were causing, each attack fuelling their satanic lust for more.

Zargot observed every move, feeling he was letting his children run riot as long as he allowed it. When he was ready to rein them in he would do so, then the power would be all his.

But the malice was splitting and spreading at a rate even he had never achieved. The ungodly masses were throwing off sprays of evil like erupting volcanoes. He had to take control now, before moving on to his next planet area.

The hybrid craft were on the move. They were encircling the earth at evenly spaced intervals. Jenny did a double switch to the moon which appeared to now be abandoned, as she couldn't believe it had been used merely as a decoy. Her brief visit proved the place was deserted, so she did a normal switch to give her chance for a full examination of the surface.

The line of impact marks took no finding as she knew exactly where to locate them. She turned her attention towards the earth, positioning herself at the first tiny crater. Then she moved along the line until she reached the end. She wouldn't have needed any fancy equipment to explain to her what was set up here, for her ideal was experienced enough to calculate it in seconds.

In earthly terms, the impact craters were not in a line as latitude would be, but in a gradual slope. Anything directed from each would cover a certain amount of the earth as it rotated, and all of them would cover the entire globe. Therefore there had to be something implanted in each which was capable of reaching the earth's surface with its power.

It hit her then. The hybrids had not been firing at the moon, but to equipment buried in it, probably charging it up. The fact that the moon had been moved slightly was a mere mishap, which was why the later impacts were shallower, the hybrids had adjusted the range and reduced the power necessary. So Zargot had set up a control of the planet from its own moon, knowing that only one side of the satellite was always pointing towards it.

One of the frightening facts that pounded her thoughts as Jenny returned to Eden was that nothing had appeared to be deposited on the lunar surface recently. This could only mean it had been previously placed there by earth people, but on Zargot's instruction. How long had this been planned? It didn't matter. Time was nothing. All that was important was that whatever maneouvers were planned, they were about to be executed.

Robert entered the cottage laden with bags, kissed Beth endearingly and asked "Where are the rascals?"

"We're here," was the chorus as both bounded into the room.

"Happy Easter everyone" Robert carefully put the bags onto the table, and distributed chocolate eggs to the three women eagerly waiting to see what he'd got.

"Oh Robert," Beth was full of emotion as she eyed her beautiful present tied with pink ribbon. "But wait," she put the box down and rushed out of the room.

"Oh Dad, it's wonderful," Margaret whispered in awe, but Lizzie was almost jumping up and down with "Oh thank you, thank you."

"Well, I'm glad you seem to like them," he teased and was immediately set upon by the two, soon to be sisters.

"You didn't think you would be left out did you?" A little voice said just behind him. Turning slowly he faced his future wife who held a small gift wrapped parcel out towards him. All went quiet as he carefully opened the package.

As he revealed the contents, Beth said "I didn't have a lot to spend, but this has always meant a lot to me. It was my grandfather's pocket watch, handed down to my father and then to me. I want you to have it."

He took her in his arms, emotion showing in his features as the tears began to glisten. Lizzie nudged Margaret and the two quietly slipped away leaving the parents wrapped in each other's embrace as though they were there for ever. Finally Robert took control of his feelings as he whispered "I know how much that means to you, and you have entrusted me with it."

Beth wiped her eyes, "But it will still be in the family won't it?" Again he held her so close as if protecting her from the world, their intense love protecting them from any power in existence.

Jenny's emotions exploded. Her Father, the Almighty One had summoned her presence.

"You are awaiting an onslaught, a personal attack, but your vision is clouded child."

"In what way Father?"

"Look at the spread of hatred, of unrest across the earth in particular, but also many of the other planetary areas. That is his way of winning. He is overcoming all the good and turning it into bad."

"And are you saying I am sitting back and letting him do it?"

Her Father waited before transmitting the reply. "You will try and say that I prevented you, but you know how great is the power of love. You can fight, but with the weapons of intensely deep feelings, affections, loyalty. All these and more. I should not have to remind you."

The consultation was over. Jenny gathered the ultimates of the upper and lower spirals, even recalling temporarily those on missions. She ordered a surge on the worst hit areas, with the instruction to keep closing the portals.

"And get as many to pray as possible. She knew that merely positive vibrations would work equally well, but some people would only understand if you asked them to pray."

The good thoughts rising from the surface would fuse with the stronger ones being generated downwards; much like the lightning streamers that Matthew had shown Jenny. With her full understanding and knowledge restored, she realized how much power was lying there dormant just waiting to be harnessed with her at the reins.

There had been another wave of UFO sightings and reports of alien abduction, some merely for publicity, and some due to night revellers being under the influence of a strong beverage.

However, one event was recorded more than most. The usual description of anything extraterrestrial was the usual grey body, slit eyes, domed head appearance which was becoming an almost everyday occurrence. The images were being transmitted by hologram from the orbiting hybrids, so there was never any evidence to prove or disprove the multitude of so called sightings.

But the J forces were no longer confined to the earth. They were taking over the craft carrying the remaining creatures and planting new images, similar to the one witnessed by Robert and Beth. These horrific sights were first aimed at a military base at a secret location in North America. Soon after, the same image was sent to Russia, followed by a string of transmissions to any area of unrest.

As soon as the accusations started to fly, the images were aimed at a space shuttle containing personnel from several nations. The shuttle crew had seen a few of the orbiting hybrid craft but been uneasy about sending reports back until they had checked them out. Recent such sightings had been played down to the extent that the astronauts had wondered if they had been imagining things.

At this point Jenny was the next in line of the upper spiral. Time to act. Taking Marie and a band of helpers she switched to as many gatherings as she could. They didn't have to be religious; in fact in most cases it was easier if they weren't. Gradually the team stirred up love, camaraderie, bonding and above all a barrier which grew in strength with the passion being generated.

They left the seeds to expand as they sped around stirring up this new wave of hope and affection, the effects soon becoming apparent. If the evil could not take hold it would shrivel and die.

This was not what Zargot needed. He had fought this daughter of Heaven before and would do so again, but on his terms. He could not cope with this influx of calm but insistent good. Before when they were locked in mental combat he felt they were on equal footing, she was fighting and he was sure he would overcome her.

Well, he could play her at her own game.

CHAPTER 27

Roger Williams was kicking himself. A previous thought had entered his head as if put there. "When you know something, you assume everybody else does."

He picked up the phone any dialled Barry Timms' number. The call was answered immediately and Roger asked if his friend could join him for a drink. It was a good excuse for Barry to give Anne, and Roger needed to talk in private. He agreed to pick the other man up straight away, and they made their way to a little country pub where they would not be overheard.

"What's this all about old boy?" Barry knew something was amiss. He'd known the detective for years and something was weighing heavily on his mind. His friend took a drink of lemon and lime and grimaced.

"Could have done with something much stronger, but better not eh?" Knowing he would have to get to the point he started "Barry, I hate to drag this up, but you know that bird that pulled you that night?"

"Oh, I was hoping that had died a death. Do we have to, I mean, is it so important?"

Roger played with his glass. "I don't know, but it's possible." He gently talked Barry into remembering the night in question, and in particular the moment as he came round after the assault.

"Let me think. She was saying over and over how good it had been, - um she was getting dressed."

"Everything." Roger prompted.

"I don't know, she was pulling her knickers back on, I think she had kept the rest on, I'm not sure, it was hazy."

"Go on, you're doing fine."

"That's it, oh wait. That's when she said that nobody must find out. She was emphatic about that, as though her life depended on it."

"Yes!" Roger took a swig of his drink as though it was now enjoyable.

"What? What's so important?"

Roger sat back and smiled. "You know in this business, you often get information in any order, then it's up to us to sort it out. Now, if you had told me this after the murder, it would have fitted quicker."

"I'm not sure I'm quite with you." Barry was still a little bemused with his friend's reaction,

Roger went on "Tell me again, ramble if you like, just let it all pour out."

Barry thought for a moment. "How good it was. Then - knickers, - then "he half closed his eyes as if picturing the scene." Then she said 'You must never tell a soul, nobody do you hear me' I was still woozy you understand"

"Yes, yes go on."

"If she finds out, I'm dead." Barry looked up. "I think I asked who, and she says something about it being alright to have her pleasures as long as the bloke didn't recognize her. Seems like I'd come to a bit faster than she planned."

"Hmm." Roger was still piecing the bits in his mind when Barry said as an after thought "She mumbled something about this not getting madam her supper but I didn't think anything of it."

The detective snapped his fingers. "That's it. Barry you're a marvel. It was there all the time."

"What was?" But the question went unanswered as Roger finished his drink, got to his feet and said "Got to go, can't thank you enough. Come on."

When he had deposited his source of information, Roger sat for a moment and put his thoughts in order.

Mandy was obviously straight, as was the other woman Deana most likely. They could go out and satisfy their sexual needs as long as they left no trail and were not recognized. Hence the hypnotic stuff which had either been their own doing, or most likely taught to them by the one in charge.

Next, it would appear that the female leader, this Zena person, liked her own kind. He remembered the call from Beth Stokes about Margaret having been approached by Mandy, the purpose obviously being to provide madam with her supper, as Barry had put it. But at that time, Madge would have already been going out without her husband's knowledge of her destination. Surely, the leader wouldn't have entertained two from the same family, or perhaps Mandy didn't realize the connection. Now that would have been interesting.

Although he was sure in his own mind of the events leading up to the cult murder, Roger knew that proving it was another matter.

He started up the car and headed home, still feeling the fatigue that would not leave him but jubilant in the fact that he felt he was closing the net.

A few offshoots of the J malice were running wild like unruly children catching victims unawares. One had caused a plane crash; another had caused the sinking of a ferry and so on. Still the forces from Eden battled to overthrow these offspring of the devil.

Fortunately the England area appeared quiet now, with little adverse activity. The country folk prepared for the approaching summer grateful that they were not caught up in some of the world's tragedies. The flowers bloomed giving the land gave the impression of Heaven upon earth. At least here peace reigned. If only the effect could be spread across the whole earth, then Jenny would have conquered her evil foe.

"How about a picnic on Sunday?" Beth's question was met with instant approval from Robert and the girls.

"Sounds wonderful," the father enthused, "where shall we head for?"

"Stratford" Lizzie offered while Margaret nodded happily. The change in this girl was so noticeable; it could almost be believed that she had never had any nervous disorder in her life.

"Need we go that far?" Beth wondered. "I was thinking of somewhere close. Save the pennies for later."

"As ever my careful little woman," Robert gave her a playful pat on the rump as she passed.

"How about round Bourton way then?" Lizzie was anxious to resolve the situation.

"Oh I love it there, can we?" Again Margaret was happy to fall in with anything as long as they were all together.

"That's settled then." Robert smiled, so contented now. "Bourton it is."

While the girls busied themselves sorting out what they would wear, Robert followed Beth into the kitchen.

"I've got to go to No.8 on Saturday afternoon. There are a couple of things the estate agent wants to sort out."
Beth turned. "Oh no. Do you have to?"
"I'll be fine he reassured her," giving her a peck on the cheek. "Don't you worry."

"Worry about what?" Lizzie overheard the last remark. As they explained Robert's necessary journey she said, "Oh I'm working Saturday afternoon Mum."
"Alright dear. Well Margaret and I can do some baking while you two are otherwise occupied, that is unless you've got to work too Margaret."
"Golly no. I'll have had enough of filing by Friday "and she laughed as she grabbed a magazine and slumped down in the settee."What are we making?"
Beth smiled. "Whatever you like."

The atmosphere was relaxed as they all looked forward to the outing that weekend.

The estate agent had a key to No.8 and had been showing people around as agreed. He had eventually found a couple who liked the place but who wanted to clarify a few points before finally deciding on the purchase.
On their visits there had been no sign of the presence which had held Robert and the ladies in its grasp, and he hoped it had gone for good, or at least until after the sale was completed.

The clients were approaching retirement, weren't short of money, and could afford to be choosy. They liked the size of the place which would be suitable for having family members to stay, but wondered if it was secluded enough for their tastes. With Robert's eagerness to get rid of the house, he considered it worth while to give a little time in order to smooth out any wrinkles, and help prove it to be what the buyers wanted.

Nothing much was left now. With Margaret's agreement, the furniture and many other items had been sold as neither wanted any reminder of the tragedy. Beth suggested leaving the curtains as it made the place look occupied, and the carpets were still in place, mainly because none of them could bother to have them taken up. If the new owners wanted to replace them, that was their problem.

It was an unspoken understanding, that once this chapter of their lives was finally closed, they could move on to the happiness they all so richly deserved.

Another positive tick on Jenny's list. For sometimes she had learned, it had more effect to sort out the smaller problems, and keep nibbling away at the undergrowth, causing the apparently bigger threats to crumble without the support they needed to survive.

But for every positive action on Eden's side, there was a balancing act from the satanic force. When one element appeared to have gained a foothold, the other was there ready to knock it down.

"It is happening" Jenny informed her ultimates. "I was waiting for another head to head onslaught, a big showdown, but that's what he expected me to do." It was becoming clear. All the so called anticipation, the hanging around awaiting the big strike or ultimatum was not going to be.

She was furious with herself for not seeing through his ruse. While she had been trying to work out his possible blackmail techniques, he had been busy, very busy. It was a little relief to realize that Eden's powers had been matching, and in many cases overcoming the evil, especially the destruction of the hybrids at the holding zone.

Her attention turned to the supposed concealed weapons on the moon which were still covering all areas of the earth. Maybe this wasn't for now, but sitting in wait for some future plan.

Roger Williams had decided to visit Deana's mother, in the hopes she may have some clue as to where her daughter could have gone. He looked at the address again. Headington, that was near Oxford, he could go tomorrow. The fatigue was really taking him over now, his head ached and he found it difficult to concentrate for long, but the burning desire to get to the bottom of this murder on his doorstep drove him with an ambition as though he was being pushed to find the truth.

The idea sprang to his mind jolting him back to full power. He had put off a job before with disastrous results. If he had moved in then, he would most likely have come face to face with this Deana and the rest. So he would not go tomorrow, he would go today. A quick glance at his watch showed it was nearly 5pm. That was alright, an evening visit was often more likely to find people at home. Perhaps he should ring to make sure of an audience, but thought it may frighten the woman off, especially if she thought her daughter was hiding something. No, he'd take the chance, and just turn up.

Then perhaps he would take the week end off and relax which was well overdue.

Saturday dawned sunny but still with the hint of a chill in the air. Beth was getting breakfast and looking forward to her beloved's arrival later in the day. Robert was going to No.8 for 2 pm and would be round as soon as the business was finished. In a lighthearted mood she switched on the radio he had given her to keep her company in the kitchen whilst making her delicious cakes.

To start with she hummed along to the music as she buttered the toast and made the tea. As she was about to give the girls a call, the local news started. She froze as she listened.

"An accident occurred last night on the A40 near the Minster Lovell turn, when a car left the road and hit a tree. The driver sustained fatal injuries. His identity is being withheld until relatives have been informed but it is believed he was a member of the local CID.
Else where today in the county........."

Beth only knew one member of the local CID, Roger Williams, the man who had believed Robert's story all along. She shook herself. There was no proof it was him yet, better wait until the name was given out.

But it was Roger. He had enjoyed a very successful meeting with Deana's mother, an amicable woman who admitted she didn't know what the lass got up to most of the time as she didn't live with her any more, wanting to be self sufficient. But she always wondered what sort of crowd she mixed with. And why had she changed her name? Roger had been interested in this for it was the first time anyone had even suggested that the girls were not using their own. "What is her name?" he asked.

"Well, it's Diane, similar, but why she changed it to Deana I'll never know. Probably wanted to sound like that woman friend, oh what was her name now?"
"Zena." Roger offered.
"That's it. Well I bet that was made up, who on earth would call a girl that I ask you?"
"Did you ever see her?" The detective was hopeful.
"Oh no. Di let it slip once and then looked as though she could have cut her tongue out. Made me promise to forget it."

After a few more little snippets of the woman's background, Roger left, anxious to get the sleep he so badly needed. He left Oxford and headed back through Witney and was soon bound for Burford.

As the thoughts churned through his mind, he was aware that he was approaching the area where the Bradley and Stokes girls had first been raped. In the headlights he could make out a figure frantically waving and pointing to the hedge. Before he could slow down, he felt the wheel turn in his hand. The car careered sideways skidding on the verge and only coming to a halt as the tree took the full impact. A scene which Matthew and Graham would have recalled with empathy.

One of Marie's helpers was there immediately to take Roger's ideal through transition, as the malevolent entity left the scene gloating in the fact that thanks to its intervention the truth would now never be found.

The news finally hit the media, and by lunchtime the whole town was shocked by the accident, which had killed the likeable young officer.

Beth rang Robert for consolation. He too felt the loss of the man who had apparently worked so hard to clear his name, but was determined that nothing would mar the family outing planned for the next day.

Again he assured her that he would be at the cottage as soon as matters were sorted at No.8.
Before he rang off he asked "How have the girls taken the news?"
"Well, that's one good thing, they are sorry of course, but it doesn't seem to have gone too deep, so I'm happy to leave it like that."
"Very wise." Robert agreed. Then almost in a whisper "Love you."

"I love you more."
"See you soon."
"Put the phone down."
"I can't."
She laughed "Well I will then, we've got work to do."
"Bye."

As she replaced the handset she felt lighter. Robert always had this effect. No matter how bad things had been, he somehow had the knack of making things seem alright. With their love, nothing could touch them.

CHAPTER 28

Lizzie got her things together to go to work. Margaret was helping to clear away the plates and asked "Do you want me to come and meet you?"
"That would be nice, but what about the baking?"
"It'll be done by then" Beth joined in, "you go Margaret?"
"Ah" a mischievous gleam crept into Lizzie's face. "She wants us out of the way in case your Dad is here" and they nudged each other as they broke into peals of laughter.
"Well, the thought never crossed my mind you couple of little imps." But try as she might Beth could not contain the smile which now covered her face.

There was a happy feeling pervading the cottage as Lizzie kissed them both and set off for the nursing home.

There was a new patient arriving the next day, and, due to a very busy week there hadn't been time to get her bed ready, so matron had agreed for Lizzie to help one of the nurses to get the job done.

"What's her name?" was the girl's first question.
"Lilian Carter. She's nearly eighty bless her, been living on her own, but since she had a bad fall she hasn't coped too well." The nurse knew this willing helper would soon be chatting to the lady, making her feel at home.

They busied about, and even when the room was completed to their satisfaction, there were always other little things that needed their attention.

Robert let himself into the empty house. As the thought of the visitation entered his mind he pushed it back as though he was repelling an unwanted guest. But although the place was void of such things, he found his attention drawn to the landing where the vision had taken been. Slowly he forced himself up the stairs, remembering that any moment the agent would be there and he would not be alone.

The entity which had drawn Williams to his death, realized there was more fun to be had by hovering around previously used territory, and although it didn't have the powers of the greater forces, it unwittingly acted as a marker for such things to home in on.

Such fiendish bodies, having realized they could not crack the Bradley/Stokes quartet en masse, were given a golden opportunity to attack the individuals now they were split. It would give them great delight to conquer such goodness and shatter all their silly little hopes and plans. Thanks to this meddling spirit, it had been offered on a plate.

As Robert approached the top of the stairs, something seemed to fix his feet to the carpet, while a severe pressure on his chest prevented him from moving his upper body. Held in that position he imagined rather than saw the vision which had threatened them previously and he realized in horror that it could come and go as it pleased, never giving warning of its approach. The area would always be a doorway through which any unwanted ungodly mass could pass.

Suddenly, he knew he was not alone as he felt protective arms around him, shielding him from the trailing arms reaching out to grab him.

"Think only of love" he was commanded from the strength and without question he projected his intense love for Beth, Margaret and Lizzie towards the being. Slowly it shrank until it was no more and the air was still.

The protective shield released him and he sank to the landing his face in his hands repeating "Thank you guardian angel" over and over again. But before he opened his eyes he witnessed a flash of a familiar face, then it was gone.

Marie took Roger's ideal, for it was he who had protected Robert and gently moved it away from the scene. He extended his gratitude for the chance to perform one last helpful gesture to this man before departing to his holding area.

"There was still so much to do." He imparted as they moved away.

"You will have many opportunities to continue" was all he was allowed to know.

The entity, thwarted by this intervention moved quickly to the cottage. It would have to split the two females for the desired effect. They were both happily preparing cake mixtures in the kitchen as it entered. "My it's gone cold," Beth wiped her hands and went to the front door expecting to see it open. Bewildered she felt the draught but could not place its source. As she turned to go back to the kitchen she was faced with the appearance of the distorted alien creature, bearing three heads and many arms, its mass twisting and dripping whilst emitting the foul smell around her until she felt she was being swallowed into the entrails.

She tried to scream but nothing came. Her body was held rigid and a pressure was being exerted from all around until she felt the life breath being squeezed from her. Gradually she became unconscious and sank into a blackness which seemed to extract her very soul.

On the other side of the door, Margaret was hammering frantically, the flour spraying from her hands as she tried to get to Beth. She had only heard a faint cry from the woman soon to be her new mother, and without thought for her own safety she knew she must get to her.

The thing was now appearing through the closed door advancing towards the terrified girl. Her hand reached out for the nearest object to protect herself, little realizing it would have no effect, but somehow a carving knife was edged towards her fist. Grabbing it she frantically stabbed at the thing screaming for it to leave them alone, hating it for everything that had happened. It thrived on this hatred, growing, towering above her until the words were placed in her brain "Fight it with love."

She stopped, and with all her will forced herself to think of her love for Beth, who she was now trying to reach.
"Fight it with love" the order came again from Jenny who had been informed of the concentrated evil attacking the family and was now at her side.

With her vast experience the daughter of the Almighty One knew that this was no little playful spirit but something she had fought before, something deadly that would stop at nothing to achieve it's purpose. She rose above the cottage seeing the extended arm of the heinous fiend reaching up to join its other tentacles. Calling on all available powers she seized the line and twisted it free of the cottage. It distorted and reshaped to enclose her within its evil wrath, and again she fought knowing this was the battle for which she had been preparing.

As Beth and Margaret found each other, protective forces guarded their ideals and their bodies with calming vibrations, and they gently nursed them back to their normal state, filling their minds with love to ease the horror left behind.

Zargot was on his way to his next victim. He had picked off the three as merely a build up to his goal, a little disgruntled at the continued intervention by the Eden forces, but that was to be expected. Now he would move in and nothing would stop him.

Jenny was still locked in combat with the evil master, but that did not deter him. He would take her along for the ride, and she could witness his pleasure in the destruction of Lizzie. This pathetic worthless creature had proved a disappointment when he had taken over the body of Vedron for the enjoyment of his sexual desires, but there had been nothing willing about her, not like the Hannah female. So it was time to use her for a little sadistic enjoyment. That should give the Eden powers something to get excited about.

His recall was suddenly switched to No.8. There was somebody familiar there as well as the helper chief and the recently departed policeman. Now he placed it. It was the ultimate known as Graham. Nothing unusual in that, he was always around nosing into things, but there was something else. He let his thought flash between Graham and recent events, until he knew. The images of Graham and Hannah were merging. He had been tricked.

As Jenny led the force fighting the mass containing Zargot's ultimate being, she felt the change ripple through the force field. Changing her tactics she pulled back and switched to the destination she knew was his target.

Lizzie was standing with the nurse by the open window in the laundry room as Jenny entered her being. Immediately Zargot took over the other innocent host and they faced each other. Jenny stirred up all the loving thought in Lizzie as protection creating as strong an aura as she could muster, but she was not prepared for the next move.

On instruction the nearest orbiting alien craft sent a beam down directed at the body of the person Jenny now occupied, searing through her clothing and burning her left shoulder. The stricken girl fell to the floor as Jenny left her body goading Zargot to exit the nurse and face her on another plain. But that would have been on Jenny's terms, and he knew he could have greater power over her by using the good people she so carefully protected.

So he left the nurse's body, but only to transfer back to the cottage and take over Margaret's form. It was Jenny's objective to get the family back together in force to act as a combined power but a thought came down from her father at this point.

"If the love they share is strong enough, it will traverse miles and time, but it will always bond together no matter what the adversary."

"Of course" she told herself, "all we have to do is stir up their emotions" and she immediately dispatched Graham back to Robert, and Matthew to join her at the cottage. Marie would take care of Lizzie, knowing the nurse would fetch physical help.

As they switched back to the cottage, Jenny knew Zargot had no intention of being overcome, for she and Matthew could not get near the place but were held off at a distance by an unseen hand. The thought came from the occupant. "So you thought you had tricked me with the blond imposter. Thought yourself so clever."

"So that's it" thought Jenny, "its revenge for Hannah."

Suddenly Jenny was sucked into the building but the scene was obviously stage managed for her benefit. Margaret was holding Beth up against the wall with a knife at her throat. Zargot laughed from her mouth. "What now you clever schemer? The answer is in your hands." Jenny entered Beth's body injecting strength to fight back and stirring up all the feelings of good she could. She yelled into Beth's mind "It's not her, it's not Margaret."

The older woman shuddered for a moment, then looking Margaret straight in the eyes she whispered "I love you Margaret, I love you very much, and I always will."

"I will kill you." the words came from Margaret's throat but the message was from Zargot.

Jenny looked at him from Beth's eyes and said very softly "No. Because there is nothing to kill. You deprive these good people of their mortal existence and you are not giving them or me a punishment, for they will live on, and they will always be together. "

Matthew, feeling the hold relinquished was in the room without delay. He saw the bodies of Beth and Margaret facing each other, the girl now lowering the knife letting it drop to the floor, but he was aware of the two powers slowing leaving their hosts, rising together still locked in silent combat.

"The fight will go on, daughter of the light." Zargot couldn't help but wish this ideal could be on his side, for although to him she would always be his absolute enemy, he had to respect her never ending fight for what she believed was right. Like him, very much like him. With this thought he departed.

"Wherever you are, prince of darkness, I will be ready for you" thought Jenny as she turned her attention to the two at her feet.

As Robert locked the door of No.8, he vowed never to enter the place again. If there was anything spooky there, the new people could deal with it, he didn't want to know.

He drove the short distance to the cottage, and as he approached the door knew that something was amiss. He flew in to find Beth and Margaret huddled on the floor, their faces ashen, tears still wet on their cheeks. Blood was oozing from Margaret's leg and the knife lay near her feet.

"What on earth happened?" He was on the floor with them.

"Oh Robert," Beth faltered "something was here, it was terrible."

"I had something at No 8 too. Was it like the other day?" Robert was looking at Margaret's wound.

"Yes, yes, only worse, it was evil." Beth shook at the reminder of it.

"Ok." What happened here?"

Margaret put her hand to her leg. "I seemed to have a knife, and I dropped it and it cut my leg."

Robert tried to raise their spirits a little. "Well it doesn't look too bad, but we'll let the doc see it, just to be sure."

"It's followed us here hasn't it?" Beth was getting to her feet and helping Margaret to a chair.

"I don't know." Robert was shaking his head in disbelief. "It's got to be something to do with what she was meddling in, can't be anything else can----"

He was interrupted by the telephone ringing, and offered to answer it for Beth for which she gratefully accepted.

"No, just a moment, I'll get her for you." As he waited for Beth to get to the phone he said "It's the nursing home."

Bewildered Beth took the call, then slowly put the phone back down. She was trembling again as she sank into the nearest chair.

"What is it?" Margaret asked.

"That was the nurse Lizzie's working with. Lizzie's been hurt, burned or something they don't know how it happened." and she burst into tears.

The hospital patched up Lizzie's shoulder fairly well, but had to graft skin from her thigh, so she would be out of circulation for a while. The cause of her injury was still a mystery to all earthly forces, but had Roger Williams still been alive he would have recognized the effects immediately.

In view of all the recent trauma, Robert and Beth decided that as soon as Lizzie was well enough they would marry and find somewhere to live right away from the area. It didn't matter now what any outsider thought, it was only the happiness of the four of them that was important. They had come through the worst experience anyone could imagine, but they would put it behind them and soldier on.

At least the emotions planted by Jenny and her team were working. But wasn't that the weapon which had scored. Love, not fear. The forces from Eden had helped these good people overcome the most powerful evil known, and they had won, so for now right had triumphed again. Jenny knew there were still remains of the J mass to be conquered, but they could be dealt with a bit at a time. They would be eroded.

Zargot hovered momentarily over Lizzie's hospital bed before returning to Zargon, his thought trail hitting Eden as it passed.

"It isn't over yet."

THE END

UKBookland
Part of UKUnpublished.co.uk
.CO.UK

UKBookland gives you the opportunity to purchase all of the books published by UKUnpublished.

Do you want to find out a bit more about your favourite UKUnpublished Author?

Find other books they have written?

PLUS – UKBookland offers all the books at Excellent Discounts to the Recommended Retail Price!

You can find UKBookland at www.ukbookland.co.uk

Find out more about **Tabbie Browne** and her books.

Are you an Author?

Do you want to see your book in print?

Please look at the UKUnpublished website:
www.ukunpublished.co.uk

Let the World Share Your Imagination

Lightning Source UK Ltd.
Milton Keynes UK
23 February 2010

150514UK00002B/1/P